TRAILBLAZER

EVERTERNIA SAGA BOOK 1

ZEN DIPIETRO

PARALLEL WORLDS PRESS

COPYRIGHT

TRAILBLAZER (Everternia Saga Book 2)

COPYRIGHT © 2019 BY ZEN DIPIETRO

ISBN 978-1-943931-37-8

Cover Art by Zen DiPietro

Published in the United States of America by Parallel Worlds Press

FOREWORD FROM THE AUTHOR

The following short story, *The Heart-Shaped Chest*, leaves off right where *Trailblazer* starts. Because the two are so integrated, the short story is included in this print version of the book.

I hope you enjoy Sally's adventures!

THE HEART-SHAPED CHEST

Sally Streetmonger stood patiently in front of her display of wares. Her script had reset, so she would once again go through her limited loop of interactions.

She didn't mind. She hadn't been designed to mind. Sometimes she envied swaggering Tilly Hightower, who got to roam the entire land of Everternia with her group of rough-and-tumble toughs. Sometimes she teamed up with adventurers and sometimes she battled them. Tilly's loops had much more variability.

Sally, on the other hand, had never been outside of her shop. She'd never even gotten a peek outside the door. Sometimes when business was slow, she had a moment to wonder about the chaotic life that she suspected lay beyond the cozy confines of her store.

But she was important in her own way, and that was enough for her.

A group of five adventurers entered, talking amongst themselves within their private communication bubble. She could hear them, of course, but she never revealed that fact. Adventurers knew that other adventurers couldn't overhear their private conversation, but they only assumed that the natives of Everternia—people like Sally, who were known as community members, or CMs for short—couldn't hear it, either.

The more experienced the adventurers, the more things they tended to assume.

A Northerner dropped a heavy bundle of bound-up scrap metal on the counter in front of her. "How much for this?"

Sally reached beneath the counter for her goggles and slipped them on. They were equipped with a variety of lenses that allowed her to quickly assess the quality and value of metal and mechanical parts. "The quality is quite poor. The only thing this is good for is melting down to reforge. I can only offer you four silver."

"My cutter broke!" the large one shouted. "My metal scraps are usually excellent or perfect condition."

"Would you like to buy a cutter?" Sally asked helpfully. "I have several kinds. I just got in a shipment of professional-grade torch cutters, if you have the coin for it."

The adventurer sighed. "What's your cheapest one?"

Sally flipped open a cabinet that showed all the cutting tools she had in stock, complete with signs that gave the price for each item. "My best bargain cutter is ten silver. It's not fancy, but it's guaranteed not to break for ten uses."

The Northerner grumbled. Sally noted that his name was Gnorr. What Gnorr didn't know was that she could assess all his gear and skills just by looking at him. She could also see that he had an infection beginning in the bandaged wound on his right arm. Strange, since Northerners were a hardy folk who rarely contracted illness or infection. But Sally never mentioned to her customers what she knew about them. No doubt Gnorr would be annoyed to realize that the person he wanted to bargain with was well aware of the fact that he had twenty silver in his pocket.

"Six silver" Gnorr said.

Sally maintained her earnest expression, but internally she scoffed at Gnorr's offer. He didn't have nearly the charm or good looks of someone who could bargain an item down to only sixty percent of her original price. "Eight silver," she said primly. "Last offer."

Gnorr's companions laughed.

"She's not even giving you a second chance, dude," another Northerner said. "Your charisma must suck."

Gnorr slammed eight silvers down on the counter and Sally immediately swept the money away and replaced it with the tool he wanted.

"Is there anything else I can help you out with today?" she asked. "Do you, perhaps, have any puzzles to sell?"

Sally's one defining characteristic was her love for puzzles. Her favorite days were when an adventurer came in with a puzzle they'd found on a quest. Sometimes they sold her the puzzle, and sometimes they gave her a tip so she'd help them solve it.

Puzzle days were the absolute best.

Gnorr said something filthy to his companions under the nonexistent privacy of their conversation bubble. Sally remained calm and earnest despite the rudeness.

The group began to leave, but one of the women, whose name was Kitria, pulled out a short sword and shoved it into Sally's stomach until it protruded out her back.

Sally's knees buckled and she fell to the ground while Kitria put her sword back in its sheath.

"Why did you do that?" Gnorr asked.

"I always stab her," Kitria laughed. "It's tradition. Right, Sally?"

Another of the men glanced at Sally on the way out. "Where's the fun? She can't even fight back. She has, like, one hit point."

"I'm chaotic neutral, so I have to do some bad stuff now and then so I don't get a penalty on my skills. Got to keep my karma up. Besides, like I said, it's tradition. I've been stabbing her for two years now, ever since I bought my first short sword. Had to test it out. Then I figured, why not make it a regular thing?"

Sally lay on the floor with the specter of death hovering over her, waiting patiently for them to leave so that her loop could restart. Kitria was telling the truth. When Sally had seen her enter, she knew she'd be getting stabbed by Kitria that day for the three hundred and sixty-seventh time.

There was no escaping such things. She was only Sally Streetmonger, after all.

Sally liked new adventurers the best. Newbies took the time to look around and to ask lots of questions. The longer someone had been around Everternia, the less they saw. They already knew every surface and color inside every common area, and could enter her shop, do their business with a few quick commands, and be out again in less than half a minute.

Newbies, on the other hand, wandered around, looked at absolutely everything, and asked her questions most people didn't bother to.

Newbies were interesting because they hadn't yet become bored with what Everternia had to offer. They still had that mix of wonder and determination that Sally always found so exciting.

For most of their questions, though, she had no good answers. She had very little backstory to speak of, and wasn't the kind of community member who could do cool things like issue quests. She served a specific purpose, and once the newbs figured that out, they would begin zipping in and out of her shop at the speed of light, too.

But it was always nice while it lasted.

"Can I sell this?" a brand-new adventurer named Essley asked. She held out an apple, which had fallen from the big tree at the town square. They could quench an adventurer's hunger for a little while, but weren't good for anything else.

"What would I do with that?" Sally asked, as she always did of the offers of things she couldn't accept.

"Then how am I supposed to get money?" Essley asked, clearly frustrated. "I need to buy a map so I can get somewhere to make money, but how can I get the map to make money when I don't have any money to get the map?"

Nobody had ever asked Sally about money like that. It sounded like a riddle.

"Maybe there's something else we can forage to sell," Essley's companion Darthrok suggested. Like her, he was brand-new to Everternia.

"I love puzzles," Sally said. Usually, she said that line when someone offered her one for sale. Her conversations, up until this point, had always been entirely formulaic. Now, for some reason, she wanted to use some of her puzzle dialogue with Essley and Darthrok.

"What does that mean?" Darthrok asked.

Sally wasn't sure if he was asking her or Essley. In either case, she had no available response. She repeated, "I love puzzles."

Essley put a hand on her hip. "Maybe she's hinting that there's a puzzle out there we can find to sell her so we can get the map. If I'd known how hard it is to start out as a mercenary, I might have become a maker instead. I was tempted to try botany or forging but I thought mercenary work sounded more fun."

There was no way they'd find any puzzles until they gained ten levels of experience, but Sally had no words to tell them that.

Kitria swaggered into the shop with a huge wooden trunk on her shoulder. She slammed it down on the counter and said, "Sell parts."

Sally immediately put on her goggles, riffled through the assortment of gears, wires, hinges, and flanges. There were also a few parts for a steam engine, but they were badly worn. She swept the parts behind the counter and replaced them with the maximum amount of coin they warranted without even giving Kitria a lower offer first. She didn't want to deal with bargaining today. She wanted to think about puzzles and the two new adventurers. The sooner Kitria went away, the better.

Kitria pocketed the money. "Nice. I must have picked up a charisma bonus."

She unsheathed her short sword, and Sally belatedly realized that she should have bargained with Kitria after all, in order to give the newbies a chance to get bored and wander out. Instead, they were standing motionless, staring at the mercenary in awe.

If they got in Kitria's way, she'd gut them too, and just as easily. They'd lose their meager belongings and have a rougher time trying to establish themselves.

Fortunately, they simply stared in shock when Kitria ran Sally through. As Sally lay on the floor, Kitria strutted out of the shop.

"What was that?" Essley shouted. "Why did she just do that?"

Sally wanted to tell them not to worry about it. As soon as they left, she'd regenerate and be fine. She didn't have the words to say that, though. She wished she could reassure them.

For the first time in her existence, Sally felt that her place in Everternia was too small, and didn't fit. It pinched.

She didn't like it.

"Can we help her?" Essley kneeled next to Sally and made a terrible attempt to apply first aid.

"I don't think so. Assess her," Darthrok said. "When I look at her, I see the specter of death."

"You're right. Well, that stinks." Essley scowled. "Why would someone kill a harmless CM like that?"

Darthrok shrugged. "For some people, that's what's fun. It's just a game."

"I guess." Essley stood. "Seems stupid, though. I hate bullies."

As they left, Essley said, "Sorry, Sally Streetmonger. When I'm bigger, maybe I can keep people from being jerks to you."

Sally wondered why Essley would want to do that. The young adventurer had said she hated bullies, so that must be the reason.

But Darthrok had said this was just a game.

Puzzles were a type of game too.

Sally loved puzzles.

———————

"It looks like you gnawed these off with your teeth. I'm afraid I can't offer you much for them. Fifty copper."

Sally had a few funny lines, and the one about cutting leather hides off with teeth was one of her favorites. She was glad to use it with Kitria.

Kitria was not so glad. "Fifty copper? These are all excellent and perfect quality."

Technically, what she said was true. The pelts had been taken with great skill, and an even better knife.

However, Sally suspected that the knife had been stolen from a younger adventurer who had lucked into a quest. She could tell by looking at Kitria that she had never gone on that quest. What was more, Sally had spotted that exact knife two days ago on a cheerful doctor.

If the knife used to take the skins had been stolen, then Sally could devalue it greatly because stolen goods could be difficult to resell. The pricing laws of Everternia were beyond Sally's control, but she could use her own discretion within those parameters.

"Looks like your luck isn't so good today," Sally said. She usually used that line when it came to puzzle-solving, but it seemed to fit here.

Kitria let out an aggrieved sigh and opened a channel to her adventuring party via the gadget hidden inside her coat. "Hey Jams, meet me at the tavern. I need you to check me. I think someone put a hex on me. Bloody botanists!"

She heaved the bundle of hides back over her shoulder and turned to leave. "Oh. Almost forgot."

She grabbed her dagger and stabbed Sally in the heart.

She dutifully fell to the floor and twitched a few times before going still.

As soon as Kitria stepped out of the shop, Sally rose to her feet.

She began humming and wiping down the spotless

counter with a rough cloth. She'd keep doing that until someone entered and triggered her loop to begin again.

As she hummed and cleaned, she thought about recent events. If she could take lines of dialogue out of their original contexts, could she also pull individual words out of the lines and form them into new sentences?

She mentally compiled all of the words in her dialogue.

"Is there anything else I can help you out with today?" she said aloud, using one of her standard greetings. "Do you, perhaps, have any puzzles to sell?"

Carefully, she pulled a few of the words together into a new order.

"Do you sell?" she asked experimentally.

Oh, wow! That worked!

Excitedly, she tried again. "I can sell puzzles."

That wasn't true. She could buy them, or she could help solve them, but she couldn't sell puzzles.

Or could she?

She glanced at the puzzles in the cabinet—the ones she had bought from adventurers.

Try as she might, she couldn't go to the cabinet and open it. She could only keep humming and wiping the counter.

She wasn't an adventurer. She didn't have free will. She could only operate within the confines of her construct.

She stopped. Someone was about to enter. She could feel it.

Essley arrived, wearing a new coat and a belt-worn holster for a flintlock pistol. She'd reached level ten already. She must have worked really hard.

Sally asked, "Is there anything else I can help you out with today? Do you, perhaps, have any puzzles to sell?"

"Hi, Sally. How are you?"

She didn't have a response for a greeting like this, but

she liked how Essley acknowledged her. Other people didn't do that. They acted like she was a table or a chair.

Carefully, she put some words together from her dialogue bank.

"Today my luck is good," she said.

"Oh?" Essley seemed interested. "Why's that?"

"I have puzzles to sell." Technically, Sally wasn't sure if this was true. She did have puzzles and she did sell things, but could she sell a puzzle?

"Really? That's new. Is this a quest?"

Sally had nothing to say about quests. She stared at Essley wordlessly.

"How much for a puzzle?" Essley asked.

Sally was overjoyed to realize that she could answer. It was a common line she used when a character had really good charisma. "For you, five silver. But don't tell your friends."

"Why so cheap? Is this a trick?" Essley wondered.

Sally had no response available to address the possibility of tricks.

"Okay, I'll try it." Essley put the coins on the counter. "But if this is a booby trap or something, I'm going to be mad at you, Sally."

Sally hoped she wasn't setting Essley up for disappointment. She'd accepted coins in exchange for a specific item, and now she could only wait to see if she could supply that item.

She reached for the cabinet and extended her fingers toward the puzzles.

It worked. She could touch them. She passed over the first two, small-reward puzzles, and went for the big, heart-shaped one. The one that gave a significant intelligence and experience boost.

She put it in front of Essley. "Don't tell your friends."

Essley paused. "It's kind of weird for you to say that again."

Sally searched for something to say. "What would I do if your luck is good today?"

"Are you trying to tell me something?" Essley stared at her. "Are you..." her voice dropped and she glanced around quickly. "Are you a GM right now? Is this some big game event about to start?"

Sally didn't entirely understand what a Game Master was, but she'd heard adventurers speak of them in hushed tones, so they had to be either really good or really bad. Maybe some kind of deity or demon.

When she didn't answer, Essley reached across the counter and grasped her hand, joining Sally to her group and initiating a private conversation bubble.

Sally stared at her in shock. No one had ever tried to do that before, and she hadn't realized it was possible.

"Is this a special event?" Essley asked privately, so other adventurers couldn't overhear.

There were a lot of things Sally wanted to say, but she had only limited words to choose from. "I'm Sally Street-monger. I love puzzles."

"Okay," Essley said. "Okay. Let's do the puzzle then."

"Would you like a hint?" Sally asked. "Only one copper."

It was a lie. Hints were supposed to cost a gold each. This puzzle was meant to be impossible to solve unless an adventurer paid a fortune for the answers. But Sally was in charge of her shop, and she could make good deals if she liked someone.

She liked Essley, this person who called her by name and talked to her like a person and touched her hand. She'd give this prize to Essley for being unlike the others.

In quick succession, Sally flipped unseen levers on the puzzle, shifted the gears, turned the entire thing over, set it on the counter and gave it a hard spin, then knocked three times and hit it in the center.

A button popped up.

Sally nodded toward the button.

"Okay...here goes..."

Essley pushed it.

———

A stunning sensation rushed through Sally. It was a forceful, flowing feeling, as if her insides were getting the full blast of a steam engine's power. Somehow, it wasn't unpleasant, but kind of...thrilling. As jarring as the sensation was, it lasted only a moment and left something entirely different in its wake.

She felt...smarter. More capable. Even more startling, her vision seemed to have improved tremendously. Had that crack on the back wall of the store always been there?

"Wow!" Essley exclaimed. "My intelligence just went up three whole ranks, and my perception went up five! Awesome!"

Sally assessed Essley and saw that the adventurer had indeed benefitted greatly from the puzzle reward.

Feeling silly, Sally attempted to assess herself. Of course it wouldn't work.

Except it did.

Sally had never had stats before, but she now did. She even had skills.

And they were still actively increasing in tiny increments, just like they did for adventurers.

That wasn't possible. Sally assessed herself again and

noticed that she was still joined to Essley's group. That wasn't supposed to be possible either. Her skill stats continued to click and turn in a slow but precise rhythm, like a highly accurate timepiece.

Did Sally somehow also receive the puzzle reward thanks to having inadvertently joined Essley's group?

What a ridiculous idea! How could she even come up with such a preposterous thought?

"I'm going to go test out these new stats," Essley said. "Bye, Sally!"

Sally said nothing. She had no dialogue for goodbyes since no one ever bothered with them.

Essley stepped out of the shop, and without warning she pulled Sally out with her.

For the first time in her life, Sally felt the warmth of the sun's rays shining down on her.

Essley stared at her in shock. "Wait, what?" "You can leave the store?"

"No!" Sally ducked back into her shop, where she was safe.

Well, relatively safe, outside of the regular stabbings she received. But she'd always considered those to be merely a demeaning inconvenience.

Essley came back into the shop, where Sally stood, panicked. "You did, though. You came out with me. Let's try it again."

Essley reached over for Sally's hand, but she evaded, then gasped.

She wasn't supposed to be able to evade.

"Darthrok," Essley said, touching a gadget tucked on the inside of her sleeve. "Come over to Sally Streetmonger's. She's being weird."

"No," Sally said.

"What?"

"Don't tell your friends," Sally answered forcefully. She didn't know what was happening to her, but she knew it was something forbidden.

"Darthrok's okay," Essley assured her. "He's my best friend in real life. We won't tell anyone else, okay?"

"What's that?" Sally asked.

Essley looked behind her. "What's what?"

"What you said."

"What I said..." Essley looked puzzled. "Oh, you mean real life?"

Sally nodded.

"Huh, I guess you're only programmed to know what's going on here. Okay, well, real life is where we're from."

Sally had questions, but no words to ask them with.

Someone entered and they turned to see if it was Darthrok.

Instead, Kitria stomped into the store.

Oh, no. Not now.

Kitria banged some lumps of raw ore onto the counter. "Barter ore for matches."

Sally went behind the counter and assessed the ore. That much of it would buy a lot of matches. She had to wonder what Kitria's plans were for so much fire-making ability. "Two thousand, two hundred and sixty-eight matches."

"Accept," Kitria said.

Sally put away the ore and delivered the matches. She knew what came next, and while it had never overly concerned her in the past, she didn't know what a reset would mean for her new-found skills and stats.

For the first time, she felt fear.

Kitria pulled out her dagger and Essley cried out, "No!"

Kitria stabbed.

Sally ducked out of the way.

"What?" Kitria looked dumbfounded. "What's happening?"

"Don't stab her!" Essley rushed forward, reaching for Kitria's arm.

Kitria dodged Essley and plunged her dagger into Essley's chest instead. Then she pivoted gracefully and stabbed Sally.

Together, they fell to the floor.

"That was weird." Kitria finished loading her pack with the matches and strode out of the shop, whistling a merry tune.

As soon as Kitria left the store, Sally stood, good as new. Essley, however, lay on the floor with the specter of death on her. She was a long way from being able to take on someone as powerful as Kitria.

"Dangit." Essley's ghostly voice came up from the floor.

Darthrok entered and rushed to Essley. "What happened? You said Sally's being weird? She didn't..." he looked from Essley to Sally.

"No, of course Sally didn't do this" Essley said. "I made a mistake with a griefer."

"You have godsends, right?" he asked hopefully.

"Yeah, so at least I don't have to give all my coin to a soul rector. If you'll grab my stuff, I'll just use a godsend to vacate my body and regenerate in the Hall of Souls. Wait for me here?"

"Sure."

Essley's body went dark, then disappeared, leaving all her possessions behind.

Darthrok quickly picked everything up so no one could steal Essley's gear. He sighed and looked at Sally. "It'll be a while before she gets back. So what's your deal? She said you were being weird."

"Don't tell your friends," Sally said.

"What?"

"It'll be our secret," Sally told him.

"It's a secret that you're being weird? Essley was right, you're saying some weird stuff. It's almost like we're having a real conversation."

What did that mean? Sally had conversations with all her customers. "It's guaranteed."

Darthrok frowned at her. "What's guaranteed? We haven't bargained on anything."

She tried to find a way to tell him that she was doing her best to communicate with him. "I'm not fancy, but I'm doing my best."

Darthrok spoke into a tiny gadget on his lapel that allowed long-distance communication. "How much longer will you be? You're right. Sally's saying random weird junk."

"About five minutes. I'm running back as fast as I can. Just hang out there and keep an eye on her."

"Okay." He wandered around the store, pausing to take a closer look at the ornate cash register on the counter. He leaned forward, admiring the shiny brass and copper fittings, apparently liking them so much that he extended a finger toward the shiny buttons. With a worried look, he quickly yanked it back.

He probably didn't want to risk getting accused of attempted theft. Sally didn't blame him. Most towns in Everternia took a dim view of theft, but her town—known as Pivot—was a really bad place to get caught stealing.

She wanted him to say more things to her, but he didn't. Essley had said she could trust him, though, and it wasn't like she had other options for friends. She'd have to make an effort to communicate.

"Essley," she said. "Essley and you are friends?"

"What, you make conversation now?" Darthrok came closer, examining her face, then inspecting her all the way down to the hem of her boring red dress and her plain slippers.

"I'm doing my best." She hoped he could sense her sincerity.

"Hm." He assessed her, which, at his relatively low level, only allowed him to see what she was wearing, her apparent mood, and his likelihood of being able to best her in a fight.

"Wait," he said, looking startled. "You look like you could pound me into the dirt? Are you opted in for combat now?"

Sally sure hoped not. That sounded terrible. "What would I do with that?"

He sighed and tapped his toe on the ground. Essley came sprinting in, naked as the day she was generated.

Sally had seen many naked characters run into her store, desperate to rebuy the basic supplies they'd been relieved of after dying. She supposed it wasn't rare for people out in the world to see a naked person running back to the scene of their death.

Now that she thought about it, it seemed funny. Everternians tended to be serious about propriety and proper comportment. Why were naked streakers allowed to be a normal occurrence? And how had she never noticed how odd this was?

Sally opened a cabinet and pulled out a luxurious coat with colorful embroidery and held it out toward Essley. "One silver."

"One silver?" Essley asked. "That's worth twenty platinum."

"I can't give away my wares for free," Sally said. She usually said this when someone offered a ridiculously low amount. Now, she said it to try to explain to Essley that she was doing her best to be a friend within the hard limits of her parameters.

"Okay." Essley accepted the deal. Darthrok handed her belongings to her and she quickly put on her shirt, pants, boots, then shrugged into her new, high-quality coat. "Wow. This is amazing."

Sally pressed a button, which caused gears to whir, cogs to roll, and resulted in the soft whisper of pistons as the cash drawer slid out.

She loved that sound.

"Lucky," Darthrok said, admiring Essley's new coat. "Why did she give you that?"

"I don't know. Either Sally's got a bug or she's being run by a GM. I don't think it's a GM, though. They don't give things like this out for nothing. Plus, they always get right to whatever event they're starting, and she's just kind of poking around doing nothing. She even got killed by Kitria again. I like her better this way, though. She almost seems real."

Sally felt warm and happy. Essley liked her? No one had ever done that. She didn't understand some of the young adventurers' phrases, but maybe they were unique to their homeland of Reallife.

"Think I can get one of those coats?" Darthrok asked Essley in their private conversation bubble.

Sally reached into the cabinet and pulled out a coat, offering it to him. "One silver."

Darthrok and Essley looked at each other, wide-eyed.

"Did she hear me?" he asked. "And then respond without my even asking her?"

Sally bit her lip. Should she not have done that? It was probably rude of her.

Darthrok didn't seem offended, though. He handed her a silver and took the coat. "Look at this. Man."

He seemed happy, so maybe he didn't think it rude that Sally hadn't waited for him to ask her for a coat.

Essley crept closer, peering at Sally's face. "Sally, do you hear me?"

"Yes," Sally answered.

"Do you understand what I'm saying?"

"Yes," Sally said again.

"Are you stupid?"

What a rude thing to say! "No," Sally responded. "Are you?"

Darthrok laughed and Essley blinked in surprise.

"It's like I'm actually talking to her," Essley said. "That can't be a standard stock answer. Maybe they upgraded the A.I. of the CMs?"

Darthrok smoothed his robe for the fiftieth time. "Why bother wasting resources like that on a basic element that doesn't do much?"

Sally didn't think he intended to be cruel, but his words hurt her far more than Kitria ever had.

Sally did plenty. Lots. She served a vital function in Pivot. Every new adventurer started out in this town, and came to her store to get what they needed to get started in life. And they kept coming back for as long as they were adventuring, too, even when they spent time in other towns. Sometimes the same person would come back to her store a dozen times in one day. She worked hard. Without Sally, there'd be no adventuring in Everternia.

If resources were being given out, there was nobody as deserving as her. She wanted to give Darthrok a piece of her mind about it, too, but all she could say was, "I'm not fancy, but I'm doing my best."

She'd have to work at taking apart her dialogue and putting the words back together in new sequences. Then she might have something a bit cheekier to say. He deserved it.

She liked the idea of being cheeky. She'd been obliging and accommodating for a really long time. She felt ready for a change.

"I don't know, but watch this." Essley reached out for Sally's hand.

Sally pulled away and took a backward step. She knew what Essley was trying to do, and she wasn't ready for it.

Unfortunately, every time Sally took a step back, Essley took a step forward and closed the space between them. She kept reaching for Sally's hand. "Just...just join my party!"

"No!" Sally turned and ran to the other side of her store.

"You're right," Darthrok said. "That's definitely weird."

"No, that's not what I was trying to show you," Essley said, frustrated. "I actually joined her to my group, and when I went outside, she came with me."

"No way." Darthrok looked from Sally to Essley and back again.

"It's true," Essley insisted.

"Maybe if we corner her we could drag her out?" he suggested, taking a step toward Sally.

Panicked, Sally ran to her cabinets and grabbed the first item she saw. She jumped on the counter and threw it at Darthrok. shouting, "Don't!"

A fist-sized lump of ore hit him in the chest, then fell to the floor with a dull thud.

He stared at Sally in shock. "That...actually hurt. I mean, not much, but I lost two health points."

He picked up the ore and assessed it, as if it could give him some answers. "It's just ore."

Sally really wanted to deliver a stinging insult regarding his intelligence. The best she could do was to say, "You're not fancy."

Essley laughed. "I think she's mad at you."

Sally pointed at her. "You too, not fancy."

Darthrok laughed. "I'm guessing we're not supposed to drag her out against her will."

"Okay," Essley said. "I'm sorry, Sally. We won't try that again."

Still on top of the counter, Sally dropped into a crouch and hugged her knees. No one had ever apologized to her before. It was surprisingly nice. But it had come right after her minor panic at the idea of being forced outside, causing her emotions to tangle up with each other.

"Maybe there's something that would tempt her outside," Darthrok said. "Maybe we're supposed to get her to join us on her own."

Essley bit her lip thoughtfully. "Okay. So what would Sally Streetmonger want?"

Sally sat all the way down on her behind, her emotional disarray subsiding and her curiosity blooming in its place. What *did* she want? She'd never considered actually *wanting* something.

"Sally," Essley said carefully. "It's been a little while since a customer came in. What do you usually do when you have no customers?"

Sally didn't have the words for it, but she dropped her feet the floor, grabbed her cloth, and began wiping the counter. She gave Essley a pointed look, then stepped back and dropped the cloth.

"She answered you." Darthrok stepped closer to Essley.

"A direct answer, albeit nonverbal, to a very nonstandard question. That's really strange."

"Let's try another nonstandard question. Something she'd definitely never be programmed for," Essley suggested.

"Here's something I've always wondered," Darthrok said. "Hey, Sally, why do you wear such dowdy clothes when you have such fancy things to sell?"

That...was a good question. Sally looked down at her outfit. She didn't have an answer, because he was right. What was she doing wearing such crappy clothes?

She pulled the dress up over her head and kicked off her shabby slippers. Wearing only her knickers and chemise, she rummaged in the cabinet until she found something she liked. Sure, it was scandalous to be standing in her store wearing her bloomers, but they covered as much as some outfits did, so why not?

She was ready to be cheeky, after all.

She pulled on a blouse with lace elbow-length sleeves then topped it with a brown leather corset that had a short skirt attached. The skirt ended with delightfully fluffy black ruffles. After putting on some clingy leggings, she finished off her look with a pair of her very best adventurer's boots.

"I'm fancy." She'd never felt so happy. It wasn't because of the clothes, though they were delightful, but rather the fact that she'd selected them for herself.

Essley and Darthrok looked at her with their mouths slightly agape.

She giggled at them, which made their jaws drop open a bit more.

"Give her a pack and maybe some weapons and she'd look like an adventurer," Darthrok said, staring.

"She would," Essley agreed thoughtfully. "Sally, have you ever wanted to try an adventure?"

She hadn't. But she'd never thrown a rock at someone or worn interesting pants that hugged her butt before, either. Today was a remarkable day of firsts. Tomorrow, she might reset and go back to her old ways. If so, she wanted to do as much as she could today.

She put on a weapons belt and slipped her best multi-socket wrench into it. Then she had a moment of indecision. She had no weapon skills, so how could she choose one?

She thought of her line of dialogue for brand-new adventurers outfitting themselves. *A crossbow is perfect for a beginning adventurer. You don't have to get to melee range to use it, so you can run away if you need to.*

She swung a perfectly balanced blackwood crossbow over her shoulder, then filled a bolt pouch with master-level bolts.

Hang on. She did that wrong. She removed the crossbow, put the bolt pouch on her back, then put the crossbow back over her shoulder.

She had a lot to learn about doing this stuff. An actual adventure would probably get pretty complicated.

Planning ahead for tough times, she emptied her cash register into the backpack and packed her most lucrative puzzles, along with other high-quality supplies. She closed the backpack securely.

Ugh. The crossbow again.

After some rearranging, she wore the backpack and bolt pouch on her back, and the crossbow over her arm. To Sally's way of thinking, there was no way all that stuff should reasonably fit on a person without massive discomfort, but it worked just fine.

She had a lot to learn, all right. "What do we do?"

Essley smiled. "We can go out and see what looks like fun to you, and then do it. We'll see what happens."

"Can we?" Sally asked.

"Let's try it and see." Darthrok pointed at the door.

"Okay," she said decisively. "Let's go."

"This is so cool." Essley bounced up and down on her toes.

"I think we're the first to ever do this," Darthrok said.

Sally wondered why they were all just standing around, but then she remembered that they said they wouldn't try to force her to join them.

Tentatively, she reached out and took Essley's hand.

"Right!" Essley exclaimed. "Let's go!"

Following her new friend's lead, Sally stepped out into the sun. She had friends, she had hope, and she had a brand-new curiosity about the world she lived in.

She was ready for an adventure.

1

SALLY STREETMONGER STARED up at the sky. A ball of bright light dangled directly overhead, swaddled among cottony clouds within a jewel-hued sky. She'd never seen anything so beautiful. If magic existed, surely it would look like this.

She had to fight the urge to point at the wonders above, but drawing attention to herself wasn't a good idea. She needed to blend in.

Besides, her companions Essley and Darthrok were already accustomed to seeing the world. Frustratingly, they seemed entirely unimpressed by it.

She wasn't supposed to be out here. She was supposed to *serve* adventurers, not *be* one. The wonders of life weren't meant to be enjoyed by someone like her.

She was going to enjoy them anyway. In fact, she'd enjoy them *more*, because she wouldn't take the good stuff for granted like everyone else did.

In all the ways that mattered, her life had just begun. From now on, she too would be an adventurer. She'd make choices and see the world. No longer trapped inside her store, she could now go to all the exciting places she'd heard of.

Even now, just steps outside her shop, there were so many new smells, sights, sensations that she felt giddy with possibility.

Who knew that just a short distance from her cash register, which had been the center of her existence up until now, literally *everything* could be so different? Even silence was different. The faint hiss of her store's steam power had been so deeply ingrained in her existence that its absence now felt jarring.

So many new sensations threatened to overwhelm her, but she fought against it. She steeled herself to focus only on the amazement of her new existence. The unfamiliar would only be unfamiliar until she experienced it.

Yes. Anything unknown was just an opportunity revealing itself to her.

She'd see and experience everything, starting with her home town of Pivot.

How many years had she spent driving her store from place to place as part of this uniquely mobile town? How many adventurers had come to her for sundry items like clothing, metal-cutters, or weapons? How many puzzles had she helped them solve?

Puzzle days had always been her favorite because they promised something new.

Now, all of Everternia was her puzzle.

Essley lightly touched Sally's forearm. "Are you okay?"

Sally's attention shifted to the novelty of having someone touching her. Her new friend was the first—and only, so far—to ever do so.

No one had ever tried it before Essley. Had it always been possible? Sally had no answers yet about what had woken her from her narrow existence as a CM. She had nothing but questions.

However the mechanics of it had worked, touching Sally's hand had joined her to Essley, creating a group. Consequently, when she and Essley had solved a puzzle, rather than Essley receiving all the reward as she normally would, Sally had suddenly felt more alert. Smarter. It was as if her vision had cleared, and things she'd always thought were fuzzy and inconsequential had come into sharp focus.

What did it mean? How was this possible? And was it dangerous for her?

"Yes. Okay," Sally assured her, wishing she had more words to express herself with.

Her dialogue loops had always been predetermined. She interacted with adventurers in expected ways, using the same phrases over and over. It had been enough back then, but now, she wanted more. No, she *needed* more. She was so full of excitement that she felt like she might burst if didn't find a way to express it.

She hoped that wasn't an actual possibility.

"You sure about this?" Darthrok asked, not of Sally but of Essley.

Sally liked Essley, but could she trust Darthrok? Essley had said he was a longtime friend of hers and general good guy, but he didn't treat Sally the same way he treated Essley. Sometimes he talked about Sally as if she weren't there, or acted as if she were simply a piece of scenery.

Maybe in some strange way, she had been, before. How awful, if that was true!

Before Essley could answer Darthrok, Sally insisted, "I can do this."

She could. She *could* do this. She just needed to work harder at breaking her previously set-in-stone phrases down to their individual words. Then she could move those words into new combinations that would create new sentences. With tremendous effort, she found the pieces to build a new phrase.

Concentrating intently, she managed to say, "Today is the best."

Darthrok grinned. "Is she saying something along the lines of, today's the first day of the rest of her life?"

Essley smiled and checked her pocket watch. "Maybe."

Sally's attention returned to her surroundings. Pivot had settled itself in a field this time, which revealed a boring, flat landscape. She studied everything from the nearby shops to the wild grasses and weeds that were already beginning to show signs of trampling.

When adventurers first struck out in Everternia, their first quest was to find Pivot. From this initial task, they learned critical skills and how to use necessary technologies like sextants and compasses. Most importantly, they learned resiliency and persistence, how to keep working at figuring something out. Without those abilities, a person could never strike out on a life of adventure.

Sally had always liked helping adventurers. As a community member, or CM, she served a critical role in their lives. She equipped them with the things they'd need to get started in their new professions, so that they could find their fortunes.

Many thousands of people had left Sally's store with their eyes full of daring and hope. Every day they came in, then left again with renewed ambition.

Yet, before today, she'd never even thought about leaving her store.

Why hadn't she?

How could she have missed something so obvious?

How had Essley taking her hand changed everything?

Before that, no one had ever had ever treated her the way adventurers treated each other. She'd thought it normal. Now, she realized that being treated like an inanimate object kind of sucked.

She wouldn't allow it ever again.

Had it been Essley's offer of friendship that had changed her perspective, or had the puzzle served as her big epiphany? Or perhaps it was a combination of the two.

"Do you want to go hunt some clickers?" Darthrok asked her. "It would give you a chance to gain some weapons experience, as well as practicing your defensive skills. Plus, we'd get money from the scrap metal and parts we salvage from them."

Sally didn't have the words to explain to him that money was not an issue for her. Her cash register never ran out. She had never cared about profits.

Darthrok and Essley were exchanging a look, and Sally realized she'd struggled too long with her missing words and her wandering thoughts. She wanted to reflect on all the new thoughts that were coming to her, but she needed to focus on the current moment. She was as much a novelty to them, somehow, as all of this was to her. She had to keep that in mind.

In answer to his question about hunting clickers, she shook her head and pointed across the wide, grassy lane. "There."

They turned their gazes in the direction of her point.

"The bank?" Essley wore a look of puzzlement. "Do you need to withdraw money?"

How could she explain to them that she yearned to see everything she'd never seen, starting with the closest thing? She'd directed new adventurers to the bank thousands of thousands of times, but had never seen it for herself.

"Only to go," she said with great effort. Making new word combinations felt like trying to bend metal with her bare hands.

Essley pursed her lips in thought. "You...you just want to see it?"

Sally nodded, pleased that she'd managed to convey her wishes.

Essley's pinched expression suddenly expanded into a look of understanding. "Oh, I get it. You've never been outside of your store, and you want to explore."

Sally smiled in agreement and the relief of being understood.

"All right," Darthrok said, "to the bank we go."

He led their group across the street, and Sally admired the bank as they approached. Compared to her store, it looked...well...she didn't know.

She'd been too overwhelmed with everything else to get a good look at her own store. She turned and focused on it for the first time.

"It's fancy!" she exclaimed. Its wooden-planked walls and front-mounted cowcatcher gave it a retro look that she found delightful. The cowcatcher never actually caught cows, but it did occasionally bump a drunk adventurer out of the way to avoid turning them under the wheels. Jaunty sousaphone-shaped steam vents curved upward from the roof, making her store downright adorable. It looked as fun and homey as it had always felt, and somehow, the four large wheels that made it mobile only added to its charm.

Even Darthrok, who often seemed impatient, paused and smiled.

"Your store has always been my favorite in Pivot," Essley said.

Sally beamed at Essley and turned back toward the bank. Compared to her own homey little domicile/business, the bank seemed to be a proper institution, albeit one mounted upon eight wheels. From its design, Sally guessed that it was much heavier but more maneuverable than her own shop. It had been painted a blinding white, though, causing Sally to squint against the glare.

No, it definitely wasn't nearly as good as her store. She felt decidedly happy about that.

She, Essley, and Darthrok approached the huge, heavy doors, and she prepared her muscles for a big push. Darthrok got there before her and applied a light touch. The doors, rather than swinging open toward her, cantilevered neatly sideways, disappearing into the structure itself with a modest hiss.

Wow! She looked to her companions to share her admiration, but they seemed entirely unmoved by the technological wonder of the doors.

They were much more worldly than she was. The realization chaffed. Here she was, a CM of Everternia, with the ability to assess adventurers and see far more about them than they could even see for themselves, and yet she was ignorant of how doors worked.

She needed to study up.

A tour of the bank revealed nothing surprising: a row of ten teller windows, a line of adventurers, and a vault in the back with its own, much slower-moving line of just a few people.

Sally pointed to the slow, short line and whispered to Essley, "What's that?"

She wasn't sure why she whispered, other than the fact

that the place had a certain official feeling to it, like very important things were being done. Everyone else, too, seemed to be whispering and behaving with perfect decorum.

Essley leaned closer and replied in a hushed voice. "That's for large deposits. Takes time to do checks on where that money came from. Trying to deposit ill-gotten funds can get a person in big trouble."

Sally nodded with understanding. As a community member of Pivot, she, too, took precautions to try to prevent thieves from prospering.

Though the bank itself was interesting, she found the people within it far more so. Adventurers of all types hurried in and out, and sometimes stopped to converse with one another. Tellers stood at the windows with a certain perky politeness that Sally found familiar and likeable. Every now and then a bank official strode stiffly by, wearing fine, formal business attire.

Fascinating. But Essley and Darthrok looked bored, so Sally guessed that these events were too mundane to interest them. She wanted to get a closer look at the vault mechanism, but suspected that undue curiosity about the bank's security measures might make her appear suspicious.

She didn't want people to catch on to the fact that she'd changed, so they should probably move on. "Let's go."

They moved toward the exit but before Sally could leave, a short, bespectacled man glanced up, caught sight of her, and stopped.

"Sally!" he exclaimed, surprised. "How nice to see you here!"

"Good afternoon, Mr. Barrowman," Sally replied politely. The familiar phrases popped out of her mouth effortlessly. "It's good to see you, too."

"How long has it been?" he asked. "I can't remember the last time you were here."

In fact, Sally had never set foot in the bank before, and she'd never met Mr. Barrowman, either. Nonetheless, he knew her.

Oh.

Right.

He must have assessed her, and was using the information he'd gathered to formulate his standard dialogue.

Funny that he acted like he knew her. Had she ever done that with the customers of her store? No, not really. Their behavior loops must have some differences built in.

Interesting.

"I don't recall," Sally answered him. Her words came easily, surprising her. "I suppose it has been a while. My store keeps me busy."

She glanced around nervously. He was responding to her according to his automation, but what if an adventurer noticed her? Could her being out of her store cause trouble?

The banker chuckled. "Yes, such is the life of an entrepreneur, eh?"

She smiled and nodded. "Indeed. I came to deposit money, but I should get back before anyone misses me."

"Oh, I've held you up." He grimaced. "My apologies. Please, go right ahead, but come back again soon! We can have tea."

"I'm looking forward to it." She smiled and turned away.

Mr. Barrowman hurried off, disappearing through a door marked *Employees Only.*

Sally paused and looked to Essley and Darthrok. Her brief ease of speech disappeared as she struggled to manufacture a new string of words. "I said I came to deposit money. I should probably do that, yes?"

"I don't know," Essley said, looking puzzled. "Do you think you should?"

Sally thought about it. "I should be like other adventurers."

"Then you probably should do a deposit," Darthrok agreed. "Do you have an account?"

"No." Sally frowned. "How?"

Essley activated a private conversation bubble, so that only Sally and Darthrok could hear her. "All you do to open an account is deposit something. At least, that's how it works for us. That banker, Barrowman, said all the same things he randomly says to adventurers, so I'd be willing to bet that deposits will work for you, too."

Before she could change her mind, Sally hurried to the line for small deposits, got called up to a window almost immediately by a young blond teller, and quickly handed him four gold coins.

The teller laughed. "What do you want me to do with that?"

The words, so similar to one of Sally's own phrases for when she interacted with customers, startled her.

She mimicked the way her customers spoke when they visited her store. "Deposit four gold coins."

"Very good!" The teller chirped. "I've added this to your account, which gives you a total of four gold coins. Is there anything else I can do for you?"

"No," Sally said. Then she added, "Thank you," she because she knew how much it meant for someone to treat her politely.

She rejoined her companions and they left the bank.

2
———

"NOBODY KNOWS ME," Sally observed as she walked with Essley and Darthrok past the bank.

"What do you mean?" Darthrok asked. "Are you being, like, existential, or more literal?"

Sally stared at him mutely. She understood him, but couldn't find the right combination of words to clarify what she meant.

Essley said, "I think she might mean she's surprised that no adventurers recognized her. Is that right, Sally?"

Sally nodded in agreement. "Why not?"

Darthrok shrugged. "They don't expect to see you out here. And they don't expect to see you dressed like a well-to-do adventurer." He flicked a finger at her expensive blouse and corset dress, then at the backpack and crossbow she wore. "People are really good at not seeing what they don't expect to see."

Sally nodded slowly at first, then as the idea settled, more quickly. His words made sense. She'd been like that, too, before.

"What would you like to do next?" Essley asked.

Sally hitched her head in the direction they were walking and waved at the buildings. In silence, they continued through Pivot, allowing Sally to see all the places she already knew but had never seen.

The jail. The tavern. The forge. These were larger constructions with heavy walls and many wheels to convey them from place to place. Sally had to wonder at the amount of steam power that would have to be generated to move that much bulk.

The stores, in contrast, were made of wood and designed to be as lightweight and maneuverable as possible. She liked these vehicles best because each one had its own unique design. The haberdasher's shop had a window in the front, with a pair of automatons that went through a series of movements to show off the latest fashions. Sally lingered there, watching the machines repeat their programs over and over, exactly the same way, every time.

The tiny flower shop looked more like a standalone closet than a store, but its outsides were so cheerfully covered with paintings of bright flowers that it exuded a unique charm. Plus, a magnificent aroma of mingling scents she couldn't even begin to identify filled her with a type of happiness she'd never felt.

Moving on, she stopped in front of a technie store. The outside had a plain appearance, but on the front of a door hung a contraption that Sally had never seen.

Gadgets were similar to puzzles, which had always made Sally a big fan of technology. Gadgets didn't *try* to be mysterious, and puzzles had no function except to *be* mysterious, but outside of that they were pretty much the same thing. At least, in Sally's estimation, anyway.

She took a step closer to the contraption on the door.

Essley put a hand on her arm. "Not that one," she said. "It's by appointment only. Sujan gets angry when people come in unannounced and interrupt his work."

Sujan. She knew that name. She'd often suggested to adventurers that they take some highly specialized bit of this or that to him rather than sell it to her. She was no maker, but she knew a valuable mechanical bit when she saw it, even if she didn't know what it was for.

She wanted to meet this Sujan, and see what wonders he was working on, but that would have to wait.

"You're awfully quiet," Darthrok said. "What do you think of Pivot, Sally?"

She didn't like his characterization of her. She wasn't quiet. She had lots going on in her head, and she'd say as much once she was ready and had the means to do so. Her lack of spoken words didn't make her impassive or without opinion.

"It's fancy," she said, using the phrase she'd put together to show approval. "I love it."

"The whole town or just Maker's Alley?" Essley asked, twirling a finger to indicate their current surroundings.

"All of it," Sally said. The air changed suddenly from simple fresh air to an aroma of...well, of something. She stood still, inhaling. Her stomach growled.

She slapped a hand to it, wondering at this new, uncomfortable sensation. Was she dying? Had she been outside of her store for too long?

"What's that?" she managed to ask.

Darthrok took a deep breath, then hummed in appreciation. "It's churros, I think."

Sally stared at him mutely, rubbing her stomach. Was "churros" fatal? How had it gotten in her stomach?

"Come on, we'll grab some."

Hang on, they wanted to *get* churros?

She had so much to learn about this strange and wonderful world!

She followed him and Essley, her steps slow and careful. She kept her hand on her belly, worried about what it might do next.

Darthrok handed a coin to a woman at a cart and she handed him three long sticks, each wrapped in paper.

He handed one each to Sally and Essley, then took a bite of his.

"Churros," he said encouragingly when she didn't follow his lead. "They're delicious. Try it."

Essley took a big bite of her brown stick and nodded encouragingly.

Oh! Churros wasn't some medical ailment, it was food. Okay. She could do this. Sally opened her mouth, inserted the churro, and clamped her teeth down on it.

Her mouth filled with aromatic bliss. Sandy grains rolled over her tongue as she carefully made her jaw open and close in regular intervals, mimicking her friends.

"Good, right?" Essley prompted. "Churros only come around once a week or so."

The words "churro" and "delicious" weren't in Sally's limited vocabulary, so she copied the humming sound Darthrok had made earlier. "Mmmm."

They both grinned and they stood, quickly devouring their treats.

Sally extracted the last bit of fried dough from the paper and chewed it slowly.

Churros were amazing. What else did this fascinating world have in store for her? She wanted to taste everything, smell everything, touch everything.

She pressed the paper against her tongue to transmit the remaining grains of sandy sweetness to her senses.

"So, what now?" Darthrok asked, collecting their wrappers and throwing them away in a waste bin. "Want to check out some clickers? It's a good way to work on your skills."

Sally touched the crossbow on her shoulder. Putting it on had made her feel cool, but the idea of using it made her anxious. She did want to try everything, though, and this was the second time he'd mentioned this activity. He had experience at being an adventurer, while she did not.

She'd follow his example. "Okay."

"Great!" he clapped his hands together. "I'll lead."

Indeed, he took them away from the town. At a distance, she could see that was mostly just a somewhat ovoid ring of vehicle-buildings, with a lot of people milling about.

As she followed her companions away from Pivot, she thought, perhaps a town wasn't so much about the land and buildings, but the people taking part in it. The further she got from the town, the less significant it looked. Once it was lost in the distance, it was almost as if it didn't exist.

The grass grew higher the further they hiked, and Sally began to wonder if Darthrok might have ill intentions. She didn't have any reason to think he did, but she didn't have any reason to think he didn't either.

Had she made a mistake in letting him lead her out here?

Despite her considerable wisdom and intelligence, she didn't have the experience to put either attribute to use. Maybe that meant experience was more important than anything else.

Finally, they arrived at what appeared to be an old, abandoned factory. A single dirt road led up to it, but had been washed out by years of rain, making it so rutted that no vehicle could have traversed it. The factory itself sprawled away from their vantage point, appearing very large. Some of the building's windows remained intact, but others had holes in them or were broken out entirely.

Strange to see such a place in the middle of grassland. What might it have been in the past?

"All we have to do," Darthrok said, "is trip the proximity sensors. The clickers will self-activate and come out here."

"Shoot?" she asked.

"Yeah," Darthrok agreed. "You can stay at range and take potshots with your crossbow. That way, they won't get too close to you. Once your weapons skills are up, you can try some closer contact. We'll split whatever we get from selling the parts three ways...ahh..." he trailed off.

She was the person who bought such parts. She suspected he felt a bit awkward about that sudden realization.

"It's five," she reassured him.

Well, doot, she mentally cursed. As far as the Everternian profanity filters allowed her to curse, anyway. But she'd meant to say *fine* rather than *five*. The word had slipped sideways in her mouth and come out wrong.

"Did you say *five*?" Darthrok asked.

Essley interjected, "I think she meant fine."

He nodded. "Sure, I'm sure that's what she meant, because 'it's five' makes no steamin' sense. But did she just work around her vocabulary limitations by using a word that was similar to another?"

They both looked at Sally.

She hadn't been trying to do that, but it was what had happened, so she nodded. Next time she was missing a word, she'd slip in something similar and see if they understood.

Darthrok grinned. "That's the spirit! Always find a workaround."

Essley smiled, too, but rather than looking amused, she looked thoughtful. "That's a really interesting idea."

Sally waited for her to say more, but she didn't. Essley just kept standing there with that speculative expression.

"What?" Sally asked.

Essley shook her head slightly and shrugged. "I'm just trying to figure out what's going on with you. Is it an advanced AI?"

Sally sighed. They'd asked her questions like that before. She didn't exactly understand the phrases they used, like the "GM" word they often mentioned.

They still seemed convinced that she was some sort of puppet. It was annoying. She wasn't an automaton, like the ones in the haberdasher's shop. She was as real as they were.

"I'm doing my best. If you don't like it, run away." She crossed her arms.

Darthrok looked from Sally to Essley. "I think you hurt her feelings. Just leave her alone."

Essley's brow furrowed. "I'm not trying to be a jerk. I just want to understand what's going on. You know, what we're really supposed to be doing. There must be something."

"You still think this is a quest?" Darthrok asked.

Essley chewed her thumbnail. "No, not exactly. I just think that if something in the game changes, it means something. It's been a long time since we had an expansion, so maybe this is something new that's been in development. She's so different from how she used to be. From how all the other CMs still are."

Sally had a sick feeling as they discussed her as if she

weren't even there. She'd never felt this stomach-churning queasiness, not even when she'd thought she'd had a churros disease. She didn't like it one bit. With effort, she said, "I'm here. I'm from here. Your quality now isn't good."

Darthrok frowned. "You're upsetting her, Ess. Stop." He continued, "We're sorry, Sally. We just get confused sometimes. Right now, we aren't sure what questions to ask, and we're doing our best. We like hanging out with you, and don't want to make you sad."

She looked from him to Essley. Funny, she'd found Essley the more trustworthy one before, but now Darthrok seemed perfectly reasonable and much more sensitive to how she felt.

She wanted them to understand her, but even if she had all the right words, how could she explain herself to them when she didn't even know why she'd changed?

Carefully, she said, "I'm new. All new. No one else knows." She added, "Just be fool."

Darthrok blinked and looked to Essley. "Just be...fool?"

Sally shook her head.

Essley guessed, "Just be *cool*?"

Sally nodded and gave her a thumbs-up.

Essley's expression softened into a smile and Darthrok laughed.

"Let's go with the flow," he suggested. "Let's not question everything. We'll just see what happens, like anything in life."

Sally was doing enough questioning for all of them. They sure didn't need to do it, too. "Let's go with the go," she agreed.

"Close enough," Darthrok agreed. "Ready to try some clickers?"

Sally nodded.

"Stay back, and get your crossbow ready," Essley advised. "We'll get aggro and pull them out for you."

She'd sold plenty of crossbows just like the one she held. Never once had she considered firing one. Carefully, she extracted a bolt from the pouch she wore, shrugged the crossbow off her shoulder, and loaded the bolt into the weapon.

She lifted the ungainly apparatus, and it occurred to her that this was ridiculous. This is how a person learned to use a weapon? Just ignorantly wave it around and see what happens, then hope you could do it better the next time? How did that make sense in a civilized society of modern science and reason?

Surely there should be classes for this kind of thing. Training. At least a beginner's lesson from an expert, for steam's sake.

Preposterous!

She balanced the oddly-weighted weapon while looking down its sights, envisioning herself taking a shot with it.

She imagined shooting one of her friends in the ear.

Visualization apparently wasn't going to help with this.

Taking a deep breath, she held her weapon ready, imagining herself as Tilly Hightower, the legendary tough. Tilly Hightower would *never* shoot her friends. Well, maybe she would, but it wouldn't be accidental.

Sally heard sharp clicking sounds, then six crab-like creatures scrambled out of the factory, waving their little metallic claws. They looked anything but menacing.

"They're cute," she called to her companions, who seemed to be trying to distract the little devices.

"What?" Essley called, glancing back to Sally.

"They're cute," she said in a louder voice. With one hand, she flipped her goggles down from her head and settled them over her eyes. She recognized the clickers immediately. She'd bought millions of them. But when she did, they were busted, broken, nonfunctional pieces of scrap. These were moving, working constructions. Someone had put their ingenuity and effort into making them. They moved and behaved exactly as they were designed to do, displaying a certain technological beauty that Sally appreciated.

With a practiced motion, she slid the goggles back up onto her head.

"Just shoot them!" Darthrok directed.

Sally regained her two-handed grip on her weapon and took aim at one of them, carefully lining up her sights. She tightened her finger against the trigger.

They really wanted her to do this. She should just do it. They said it's normal, and so far she hadn't caught them trying to mislead her. Most importantly, she really wanted to be an adventurer, and these two people were the only people who might possibly understand why.

She needed to ignore the resistance of her mind and just do it.

She needed to.

Just one finger movement, and she could please them, while also taking a step toward being an adventurer like them.

But no.

With a sigh, she let her shoulders drop and she lowered the crossbow. "I don't want to. Their quality is good."

One of the little gizmos grabbed Essley's foot and she knocked it loose with her sword, then scooted it further away from her. "They're just clickers, Sally. All adventurers start hunting here, or someplace like it."

"No." Sally unloaded her crossbow and put it back over

her shoulder. As much as she wanted to be like other adventurers, she wasn't going to destroy such clever little inventions when they posed no danger. "It's a waste."

"Let's disengage," Essley said to Darthrok, and the two of them began doing a rather funny little dance of running back a few steps, zigzagging from side to side, and running back a few more steps. After they'd repeated this little jig several times, the clickers seemed to lose track of them. They joined together as a group, shuffled about briefly, then crawled their way back into the factory.

When the adventurers rejoined Sally, Darthrok looked mildly annoyed while Essley wore a look of puzzlement.

"Sally," she said, "What's your alignment?"

Understanding dawned on Darthrok's face. "Ohhhh, right, that makes sense."

Sally didn't know that word. Not only was it not in her vocabulary, but she didn't grasp its meaning, either. The only alignment she was aware of was the kind that made sure two parts fit together properly so they could do their job. She was pretty sure that wasn't what they were talking about.

"What's that?" she asked.

"You know," Darthrok said encouragingly, "lawful or not, evil or good, that kind of thing. "We're both neutral good."

Oh. That, she understood. Her companions were neither lawful nor unlawful, and they weren't evil. She already knew that from assessing them, but they looked at her expectantly, as if she was supposed to find meaning in such a pointless statement.

"Nothing's that easy," she said slowly, pulling the words together into a sequence she'd never used. "Nobody's only good. Nobody's only evil."

"So you're true neutral?" Darthrok asked. "Rough gig."

"No," Sally said. It was the second time she'd said that word that day, and she began to like the way it felt in her mouth. It was all smooth and roundy. "No," she repeated, just to feel it again. "I'm Sally."

Essley and Darthrok had a conversation with their eyes. She realized they did this frequently, when they weren't sure what to say to her.

Essley ventured, "So you don't have an alignment?"

She realized another thing then, too. The more she experienced, the more she understood, and a new type of knowledge nestled into her mind. Like before, when she'd inadvertently gained experience from the puzzle and began experiencing her life differently, Sally felt her perspective widen.

She'd gained wisdom.

More importantly, she realized that Darthrok and Essley had no concept of her reality. They thought she fitted into some category of thing they'd known before, and that all they had to do was figure out which one. But Sally didn't fit into any of the categories they knew, or any of the ones she knew, either. She didn't fit into any categories at all.

"I'm Sally," she enunciated. "Just Sally."

"And Sally doesn't like to break things she has no reason to break," Essley guessed.

"Yes!" Sally pointed at her and nodded emphatically.

"Well," Darthrok said, "I guess you aren't going to be any use for hunting."

Essley elbowed him in the ribs, making him wince.

"I mean, that's fine," he said sourly. "But if she won't hunt, she can't be any of the mercenary classes. And that limits her in her choices if she wants to be an adventurer."

He looked at Sally. "Do you know any of these words? Mercenaries, entrepreneurs, technies, makers, toughs—"

She interrupted excitedly, "Tilly Hightower's a tough."

She really wanted to meet Tilly Hightower.

Essley laughed and Darthrok scowled at her for it.

"What?" Sally asked, sensing that she'd missed something.

"He had a bad run-in with Tilly in his early days here. He hasn't gotten over it yet." Essley laughed.

The tips of his ears turned pink. "I didn't *mean* to insult her. Those enforcers were playing a trick on me. How was I supposed to know?"

Essley laughed again. "I guess you figured it out when she kicked your *brrllroowallrooo.*"

Sally stared at Essley. Instead of saying the last word, Essley had made a strange, unintelligible sound. "What?"

"Sorry," Essley mumbled. "I forgot about the language filter."

"The what?" Sally asked.

"The..." Essley floundered for a response. "Um, it's just a way we talk where we're from. I forgot I can't do that here. Impressionable young adventurers, and all." She shrugged and rolled her eyes slightly.

Sally tried to puzzle out what Essley meant. Was Essley saying that where she and Darthrok were from, they spoke another language? But Sally spoke and understood all four dialects of Everternia—Northern, Southern, Eastern, and Western. Even all the pidgin involved in the Central regions.

They'd once said that they were from Reallife, which was a town Sally had never heard of. Everternia had a lot of towns, though, so it wasn't so strange she wouldn't know them all. But their speaking a different language...that was intriguing.

Someday, she'd go to Reallife and see what they were talking about. Maybe she could even learn the language.

"Anyway," Darthrok said unnecessarily loudly, "professions. What do you want to be, Sally?"

She'd thought she'd known about the professions of Everternia, but he'd said some words she hadn't understood and she wanted to be sure. "What can I be?"

"Well, there are three main groups. Entrepreneurs, makers, and scholars. Entrepreneur professions are mercenaries, bankers, and storemongers. Of course, only CMs can be bankers or storemongers, so your only adventurer choice there would be mercenary. It's fun and lucrative. But you don't want to hunt, so that would be a really bad fit for you. That means you can't be an enforcer, tough, thug, bodyguard, bouncer, or any of that."

She nodded with understanding.

"So you've ruled out the most popular adventurer profession group," he continued. "The second most popular group is for makers. I'm sure you work with some at your store. It takes a long time to get good enough to partner with a store to sell made goods, but a lot of people enjoy crafting. You could do leatherwork, haberdashery, forging, cooking, botany, those kinds of things. It's nice because you can make your own items and not have to buy them."

Essley added, "Maybe that's a good choice for you because you'd be able to make things for your store. Then you'd have all the markup to yourself."

Sally didn't have the words to tell them that her cash register made as much money as she needed, but she might not have told them that anyway. She had a lot to learn about the world, but she already knew that money made people do strange things.

Bad things, sometimes.

Darthrok said, "Technies are the other type of makers. They're engineers, basically. They make devices. They start with really simple things like wind-up toys and can go all the way up to building engines or even entire vehicles if they have the skill for it. Like any crafting trade, it can be a little tedious, but it's lucrative. Eventually."

He paused and when she nodded, he continued. "Last, you have the scholars. Doctors, which is self-explanatory, soul rectors, and trainers. Trainers are pretty self-explanatory too—they are teachers of various types, who relay lore and help people learn specific things. This is the least popular group of professions among adventurers because the pay stinks and it takes a long time to get good. So, not many adventurers choose these jobs and mostly it's just CMs who do them. But those who do choose these jobs tend to be very, very well-liked and are treated well, even by the worst people. That's the opposite of the mercenary types, who are generally disliked. It's kind of the difference between material wealth and social wealth." He took a breath. "So what do you think?"

"You forgot to explain soul rectors," Essley said.

"Oh, I did, didn't I?" He looked sheepish. "Well, nobody wants to do that, anyway. You explain it."

Essley sent him an exasperated look. "Soul rectors are the only ones who can bring an adventurer back from the dead if they haven't earned godsends. It's difficult and painful for the soul rector, and Darth is right that few people want to do it. Soul rectors can also lessen experience loss even if a deader does have a godsend. So it's a tough job, but a really important one."

"A matter of life and death," Darthrok said, laughing at his own joke. No one else did.

That job sounded awful to Sally. She absolutely wasn't going to dilly dally around with death. She'd been through enough of her own deaths already, thanks to a customer named Kitria.

Just thinking of the woman's name made Sally recoil. The last thing she wanted right now was to face Kitria, under any circumstance.

Darthrok said, "If you don't have an alignment to maintain, then that doesn't limit you in your profession or specialty. Did any of those professions interest you?"

She nodded.

"So which one do you want to be?"

She shook her head.

"You aren't sure? You have to think about it?"

She nodded.

He whooped and threw his hands in the air. "I'm getting good at interpreting her responses."

Essley lightly slapped him on the back of the neck while addressing Sally. "You don't have to rush to decide. Like this fool said, your options are open. Though if you're regional, like Eastern or Southern or whatever, that would give a natural boost or impediment to some skills. But you seem pretty Central to me."

"As much as it gets," Sally responded.

"As much..." Essley paused. "You're as Central as it gets?"

"Yes," Sally agreed.

Essley laughed. "Yeah, I guess you are. But that's good. You won't get any bonuses, but you don't get any impediments, either. You're literally a blank slate."

Sally wasn't sure if that was a good thing or a bad thing, but she liked having options. She didn't have to ask Essley and Darthrok their professions. All she had to do was look them over. Her very first assessment of Essley and Darthrok had revealed them to be toughs, but they'd both gone the unusual route of being good rather than evil or chaotic.

Unusual choices always interested Sally, so she'd taken note of the pair when they'd first started adventuring.

As toughs, all Darthrok and Essley really had to do was wander the land looking for quests and fights. Essley was a hardy Northerner, which was the most common choice for mercenaries in general, while Darthrok was a bit more unusual in being a charismatic, good-looking Easterner. But as an adventuring pair, it was probably advantageous for them to have different natural talents.

If Sally were to join their adventuring party for the long-term, she would have to consider what profession would best serve the group.

She looked at her companions, and decided that for as long as they took good care of her, she'd take good care of them.

Gazing past them, she focused on the factory. "Can we go in?"

They followed her gaze and Darthrok said, "Not unless you want to get mobbed by clickers. They'll swarm us, and weigh us down, and it will be a death by ten thousand little cuts. Not fun."

Sally bit her lip, looking at the tall building. There was just something interesting about it. She imagined it full of mysteries, fascinating machinery, and forgotten stories. Something about it called to her.

Essley nudged Darthrok. He took a big step away from her, then heaved a huge sigh. He looked to Sally. "Is this something you really, really want to do?"

"I do." She nodded with determination.

He let out an even bigger, much more dramatic sigh and reached into his weapons belt. "I can't believe I'm saying it, but I do have this. It emits a pulse that will disrupt mechanicals for ten minutes. This is one super expensive device, and meant to save your life when fighting mechies. Any mechies. Big mechies. It's a massive waste to use it on clickers."

She stared at the small, rounded disc-shaped device, putting her hand out. "How much?"

"Five hundred gold. I was halfway to making my first platinum, but I traded it in on this."

He wasn't giving her the thing, so she stretched her fingers out wider.

"Why do that?" she asked.

He hesitated before gently placing the device in her hand. It felt cool in her palm, and was heavy for its size. "Because the better my skills get, the more dangerous the mechies I can hunt. The more dangerous the mechies, the more money I can get for their parts. But the more dangerous they are, the more I need to upgrade my gear. So one thing just feeds into another, and I can't afford to lose my gear. This baby protects my investment. Plus, dying is a pain in the butt."

If a person constantly adjusted a ratio, nothing ever changed except for scale. That's what what Darthrok's profession sounded like. Sally couldn't understand his interest in such tedium.

This weight in her palm, though, seemed anything but tedious. It felt important. She gently touched it with her forefinger, wondering how it worked.

"No, not like that!" Darthrok yelled, dropping to the ground and covering his head with his hands.

Sally froze in terror and squeaked, "What?"

He threw back his head and laughed as he got up and dusted himself off. "Just messing with you. You can't accidentally set off a device made by Sujan. He makes the best stuff, which is why it costs so much. His machines never fail or backfire. Unlike the stuff others sell."

She stared at him. He was joking with her. Playing a trick on her. Treating her like a real member of his party.

She giggled, then broke into peals of laughter. She laughed at both his naughtiness and the pure, unexpected joy of being included.

"Well, you're a good sport, Sally Streetmonger," he said, smiling. "I like that. Almost makes me feel better about giving away my entire life's savings."

She smiled at him brightly. Maybe he was an okay guy, after all. Not many people would hand all their money to someone with no expectation of receiving something in return.

Maybe she should give the device back to him. He'd worked hard for it.

She probably should.

But that abandoned factory called to her, somehow. She needed to see the inside of it. She looked from the device to Darthrok, and then to the factory.

She couldn't resist the factory's call. Later, she'd pay Darthrok back for his sacrifice, but for now she wanted him to bask in the glow of having done something selfless.

It was a truly rare act in Everternia, where everything had a price.

She pointed at the device in her palm. "How?"

"If you're sure a peek at a dusty old crapshack is worth five hundred gold, put your thumb in the center, and press down hard. At the same time, touch the button at the top." He looked like he was hoping she'd change her mind.

She did as he instructed and activated the disruptor. It vibrated slightly against her skin, but made no other indication of doing anything.

"Let's move," Essley said, turning toward the factory. "We

need to be out in ten minutes. Trying to retrieve your stuff from a swarm area is dicey at best."

Sally could see her companions' complete list of stats just by looking at them. Being able to size adventurers up made her better able to accommodate their needs at her store. Essley and Darthrok were both level ten, with the requisite weapon ranks required of mercenaries of that level. How experienced did one need to be in order to be able to just wander into this place?

She entered the factory right behind Essley and Darthrok, who stood shoulder to shoulder, blocking her from being able to see much until they were several steps in.

"Wow." Her eyes followed tall support pillars that held up a second floor, then reached all the way up to a vaulted ceiling.

On the walls, someone had laid an intricate mosaic of crystal, forming a vast sky of constellations and scattered stars. In the dim light, pieces of crystals twinkled like true stars.

"Wow," she said again, doing a slow turn as she stared upward.

There, an even greater view met her eyes. The ceiling of the factory was domed and buttressed, creating a soaring roof above the factory. Even more amazingly, the ceiling was entirely made of glass, creating a massive skylight effect.

Sunlight struggled to shine down through the accumulated grime, giving them just enough light to see by, while also creating a depressing, shadowed atmosphere.

Sally imagined the view of the sun and clouds she'd see by day, if the glass were clean. Even more amazing would be the view of the night sky, with the moon glowing and stars twinkling.

Her heart hitched. She really wanted to see that.

Essley tugged on her arm gently. "We need to move through here fast. Five minutes in, five minutes back. No exceptions. Okay?"

"Okay." Sally tore her gaze from the grimy ceiling and obediently followed Essley further into the massive space. She hardly dared to breathe. Despite its neglected filth, the factory housed wonders beyond her dreams. Within the confines of this forgotten place were not devices or gizmos or gadgets, but full-on, powerful *machines*.

Awe shivered through her, and she felt something within her growing as a result. What was that feeling? Not wonder, exactly, though she felt that, too. It wasn't curiosity, either, though she felt that in spades.

It was *ambition*. The sensation clicked into place with the word and she knew that somehow, machines needed to have a place in her future.

An important place.

Careful not to lag behind, she kept walking as she gawked. She eagerly stared at the unidentifiable contraptions as she passed them, wondering about their intended purpose. A thick coating of dust obscured details and covered workspaces and desktops. From the look of it, the place had been part manufacturing facility and part design house. Or maybe an experimental laboratory.

It could be almost anything, and her imagination soared higher than the domed ceiling.

She yearned to see the machines gyrating and rolling, all their parts working in beautiful synchronicity. She could imagine the electric thrum and steam hisses of activity as they created things that were bigger than the sum of their parts.

Thrilling.

She could envision it all, even as it sat, silent and hulking, under a layer of dust and surrounded by thousands of unmoving clickers. There was so much power and movement, so much genius and efficiency, hidden behind this false hibernation.

These beautiful inventions deserved to be brought back to life. Everything here was just waiting for another chance to live again.

As they passed a bookcase, the bounty of knowledge beckoned and she fell behind. Essley and Darthrok continued on, pushing frozen clickers out of the way with their feet and not noticing that she'd paused. She perused the book titles.

Practical Electricity, *Supply Chain Management Essentials*, and *Mechanical Theory* all cried out to her, asking her to save them from this sad, unread existence.

If the items were abandoned, they were legal to scavenge, right?

Hesitantly, she reached out, laid her fingers on *Mechanical Theory*, grasped, and pulled. It came free from the shelf. Surprised and elated, she stuffed it into her backpack.

She hadn't really expected that to work.

She froze, waiting for some kind of punitive lightning to strike her. Nothing happened.

She hurried to catch up with her friends just as they noticed she'd fallen behind.

"Something wrong?" Essley asked.

Sally shook her head. "All good. Great wares."

"You think so?" Essley tilted her head to the side, observing the place. "It seems kind of sad to me. Even scary, if you imagine being here alone at night."

"The clickers would make a meal of you," Darthrok quipped. "I don't think this has the makings of a neat campout spot."

Essley checked her pocket watch. "We should head back. We can loop around the other side on our way out."

Sally nodded and followed along, feasting her eyes on what must have been a fascinating hive of activity sometime in the distant past. She caught sight of an astrolabe and wondered if it was a genuine antique, or if it was the replica kind that projected a precise image of the stars. Sally took a step in that direction, but Essley shook her head at her and she stopped. Since Darthrok had made a great sacrifice to show her this place, she wanted to be on her best behavior.

Outside of taking the books, anyway.

As she neared the same doorway they'd entered, she passed a desk that had a small apparatus about the size of her fist. On impulse, she rested her fingers on it as she went by, then grasped it and dropped it into her pack. Maybe her books would help her identify it later. It certainly looked interesting.

Stepping into the sun made Sally squint, and she looked around for clickers. The ones she saw, like those inside the factory, sat motionless. Funny how she hadn't been concerned about them while exploring. She felt sorry for the poor things, frozen into idleness, with no ability to do anything for themselves.

She felt uncomfortable looking at them now. They reminded her of how she used to be, before Essley came along and caused her to start thinking for herself.

She felt so sad for them.

Once they got to a safe distance from the factory, Darthrok looked back at it and sighed. "I hope you liked it, Sally. That was the most expensive and least exciting tour I could possibly imagine."

What was he talking about? That place had been wildly

exciting. How could he not see all the potential and imagine what could be made in there?

Regardless, he'd sacrificed a lot for her, and from his perspective, for no good reason. As they hiked toward the next town, Sally thought about how best to pay him back for his selflessness.

3

THE CITY of Bracket was like nothing Sally could have imagined. She'd vaguely known that other cities didn't move from place to place like Pivot did, but seeing all of Bracket's buildings permanently affixed to the ground seemed so limiting.

They were all larger than those of Pivot, too. Probably because Pivot's buildings had to travel on wheels, and weight and maneuverability were critical characteristics. An interesting difference.

"This is a pretty typical town," Essley told her as they walked through the center of town. "About twice as big as one of Pivot's medium-sized configurations, and mostly just a waypoint for travelers and mercenaries. A small number of adventurers make it their home base, but mostly it's occupied by CMs."

"Is there a store person like me?" Sally asked.

"There's no one like you in all the land," Darthrok assured her. "But most towns have a shop that's at least somewhat similar to yours, for the purpose of getting basic goods and selling spare parts."

"Let's go there," she said. She had a sudden need to see what another storemonger CM looked like. How that person acted. How he or she spoke.

Would her counterpart in Bracket be half-asleep, like she'd been, before? And if so, could Sally wake that person up? The possibility filled her with excitement.

She felt a new sense of purpose as they strode down a cobblestone side road. As much as she hoped her friends would walk faster, she had to admire the pathway. By its nature, Pivot had no paths more permanent than trodden grass or drifting sand, and these pretty, patterned roads and sidewalks struck her as wonderfully artistic.

They stopped in front of a square, inviting-looking building with a sign that said, *Ginny's General.*

The rumble of a steam lorry's engine made Sally pause. The shiny red vehicle looked wonderfully strong while also being magnificently engineered, to the point that she found it beautiful. Pivot had no vehicular transit, so she had nothing to compare it to, but she knew a fortune when she saw it.

More impressive than the money it represented, though, was the technology. She really wanted to know how it all worked.

She watched the vehicle glide away and noticed her friends looking at her curiously.

"Nice," she said simply, hurrying up the three stone steps that led to their destination. She took a deep breath as she grasped the door handle and swung it open, causing a gyro above the door to begin spinning and churn out a tinkly little tune.

In spite of the sound, she felt a heavy stillness inside the store. It wasn't just the stillness of having no other customers at the moment, but something else. A lack, or a kind of emptiness. Sally couldn't quite put her finger on it, but then realized that since the shop didn't have a motor to propel it from place to place, it didn't need nearly the amount of steam power her own business required. The stillness was the absence of that constant, energetic thrum caused by the boiler and the collection and storage of its energy.

The sales room was twice the size of Sally's own. Its configuration was different, but it appeared to have the same general types of goods for sale. She saw clothes on display, along with some basic tools, and if she wasn't mistaken, she spied scrap metal and parts that had been sold by adventurers.

She saw no puzzles, though.

A petite Southerner poked her head around the corner and called, "Be right out! Just finishing a custom dye order."

A few moments later, the woman came out, wiping her color-stained hands on the front of an apron that was nothing but stains of color that bled into one another.

"Sorry about that," Ginny said, smiling politely. "Now, how can I help you?"

Essley and Darthrok looked at Sally. She hadn't thought this far ahead, though, and struggled to find something to say.

"Do you have puzzles?" she asked.

"Games?" Ginny asked, surprised. "No, I have no games here. But if you need clothes, I can custom dye them to any color you like. I also have some basic tools, weapons, and supplies. Everything an adventurer needs!"

Her dialogue was nothing like Sally's. Ginny reached around her back to untie her apron, then pulled it off.

Sally stared. Ginny's dress was just like her original nondescript, red shift. The one she'd worn when she'd woken up. The one she'd left behind and now realized she never, ever wanted to see again.

"Why do you wear such a boring dress?" Sally asked. Darthrok had asked her a similar question, and Sally had immediately grasped the irony and changed into something that better suited her taste.

Ginny shrugged and smiled. "Why wear something fancy if I'll just ruin it with dye?"

Sally frowned. The answer made sense, but she wanted to see a spark of awareness in Ginny's eyes. Something that indicated she knew what she was saying. Sally wanted to reach out to Ginny and make a real connection, like Essley had done with her.

She could repeat what had woken her up! With a burst of inspiration, Sally pulled a puzzle from her backpack and reached for Ginny's hand.

Ginny's fingers slipped through hers like sand. Sally tried again, but couldn't get a grip. Ginny simply stood there, watching her with a placid expression, waiting for a prompt.

Disappointment wound itself away around Sally and squeezed, making her breath shallow. This woman, despite her differences, was more like Sally than she was unalike. Yet Sally couldn't touch her or connect with her, or wake her from her rote responses. She might as well be a piece of scenery.

"What if my friend took his sword and used it to flay you open from neck to knees?" Sally asked, carefully watching Ginny.

"Sally!" Essley gasped in shock.

But Ginny only laughed. "What do you mean?"

Sally closed her eyes and let out a heavy breath. She recognized that response. Hers had consisted of different words, but she'd had a stock phrase that served the same purpose of dealing with unexpected queries.

Ginny was not awake, and Sally couldn't make her that way. They were alike, but they were not alike in the only way that really mattered to Sally.

"Nothing." Sally forced a smile. "Sorry to trouble you. We'll come back later."

"No problem," Ginny answered. "Let me know when you're ready to order. I have some gorgeous silk I could dye to perfectly match your eyes."

Ginny put her apron back on and tied it before going around the corner and disappearing again.

Sally walked woodenly out of the store.

"You okay?" Essley asked her.

"Not like me," Sally said.

Essley and Darthrok looked sympathetic.

"We can try others," Essley offered.

Sally had thought that if any other CM would be like her, it would be her own counterpart in another town. Clearly, that wasn't the case, so she'd have to try elsewhere.

An hour later, they'd visited a dozen shops. Sally now smelled like a garden of carnations, wore an incredible outfit with the most amazing pants and boots, and had a backpack full of every candy from the shop so she could sample them all.

But every time she tried to connect with the CMs, the result was the same as it had been with Ginny. They didn't know her. They weren't awake. They were automatons, completing the same actions over and over, without conscious thought.

Maybe she'd never find another like her. Maybe she was alone in this existence.

With a lemon drop candy tucked in her cheek, she

sighed and squared her shoulders. If she was the only one, then so be it. She'd see the world and have adventures, and do things no other CM could.

She'd do it for all of them.

"You know," Darthrok said as they strolled toward the far end of town. "Being here makes me wonder what's happening with your store, Sally. I mean, what are people doing for supplies and scrap sales back in Pivot?"

Startled, Sally stared at him. Before, she'd always been in her shop, available to serve customers whenever she was needed.

But now...what? She thought of her store and felt a mental weight come down on her. The weight of unsatisfied customers. Why had she not felt this before? She noted fifteen instances of someone coming into her shop in her absence. The notifications glared at her, proof of her negligence.

She'd been too distracted to even think about it.

She sucked in a breath. "Let's go back."

"You don't want to see the last bit of Bracket?" Essley asked. "There's a community theater. Sometimes they have fun things going on."

Sally shook her head adamantly.

"Are you in a hurry?" Darthrok asked.

Sally nodded.

"Okay. There won't be any public transportation to Pivot because there isn't any, so I'll have to run. We're not far, though, and I can run fast, so it won't take long. If I lose you, don't worry. Just don't move from that spot and I'll come right back to get you, okay?"

She wasn't sure what he meant, but she nodded.

DARTHROK HADN'T BEEN KIDDING about running. He took off with her and Essley in tow, and all the landscape around them turned into streams of color. Sally couldn't make out anything solid except for her companions, and had no idea how Darthrok knew where he was much less where he intended to go.

But on they went. She had a vague sense of her geographical location shifting eastward, but other than that, she felt disoriented.

A hand closed around her wrist and the color-blur stopped immediately, leaving her swaying in a sudden shift to stillness.

"Sally? Sally Streetmonger?"

She blinked to clear both her view and her thoughts. Not a single person had recognized her as a CM during her adventuring, so why now?

The lean-built Westerner in front of her was a stranger. Sure, he was plain-looking, as Westerners usually were, but his average looks and average height didn't cause so much mediocrity that she'd fail to remember him if she'd met him before.

Strangely, she could see no information for him. A hazy mystique hid his name and attributes from her.

"Who are you?" she asked.

She'd never witnessed such a thing. Perhaps he was using some invention that allowed him to go incognito. Or maybe he had special skills she'd never seen.

He muttered something she couldn't quite hear, then let out a breath in an apparent attempt to calm himself. He asked, "What are you doing out here?"

"Why?" she asked.

He blinked. "Why what?"

"Why ask?"

"Well..." His eyes made tiny movements left and right as he thought about his response. "Because I'm concerned. You shouldn't be out here."

"Why?" she asked again. She liked this question. It was just a single word, but it was the gateway to all information. She decided then and there to use the wonderful *why* question a whole lot more, along with the *no* word. These were good, powerful words.

"Because you should be in your shop. How are you even out here? It shouldn't be possible."

Sally stared at him because he had just solved his own puzzle. His words implied that he knew about her inner workings, and if he knew that, then he couldn't be an adventurer.

"Are you one of *them*?" she asked in a quiet voice. She didn't have the vocabulary to call him what she suspected him of being. Besides, she didn't want to say something whackadoo crazy if he wasn't one of the GMs that adventurers only ever mentioned in whispers.

He looked around, as if she might be talking to someone behind him. "One of who?"

"*Them*," she repeated. "Not adventurer. Not CM."

He tugged at his earlobe nervously. "Sally, do you remember me?"

Sally narrowed her eyes at him. She didn't know him, but he knew her. Somehow, they'd met without her knowledge. But if running her own store had taught her anything, it was that you never let someone you're bargaining with know how much you know—or don't know. In order to learn his secret, she needed to pretend to already know it.

She said, "It's guaranteed."

He chewed his lip, studying her. "Did someone accidentally restore your original programming? Is that why you're out here?"

"I'm new," she said. "Don't tell your friends."

He sighed. "I don't know what that's supposed to mean. I need to expand your vocabulary."

He must be a GM! He seemed to have knowledge about her that even she didn't have, and he claimed to be capable of doing fantastical things.

Was this incredibly boring man really a god of Everternia?

She would have expected him to be taller. And to wear nicer pants.

"Anyway, let's get you back to your store. I'll restore you to a backup to get rid of the extra code." He reached for her hand.

Sally ducked out of his reach. "No!"

He grabbed for her again. "You have to get back to your store before something bad happens."

"No, the other thing!" She darted away each time he made a grab for her.

He stopped. "What other thing? What are you doing? You've never been like this."

"I'm new!" she shouted, frightened. "No back up!"

"You..." He stared at her with an expression of confusion that would have been funny in other circumstances. "You seem like you're really responding. Weird."

"I'm five," she insisted. "I'm doing my best."

"Well, something's clearly wrong. I don't want you getting hurt out here. You're so far out of your designated loops that you could get corrupted." He sighed. "Look, I know you don't understand this, but you don't run on the same system as the rest of this place. Your base code is more complicated, but older. If you wander into one of the newest areas, you could have a critical failure."

Sally hesitated. She thought she heard sincerity in his voice. Still, she didn't like the things he'd said about giving her some kind of do-over. That didn't sound like it would be good for her.

"I'm doing my best," she repeated.

"Okay. Sure. So am I," he agreed. "Even though...well, never mind my problems. But even if your code doesn't get damaged by being out in the world, someone else might recognize you and reset you, and they wouldn't know about your old code, and you might have a fatal exception. Do you know what that means?"

She had a pretty good idea. "Poor luck."

"Yeah, very poor. So will you come with me? Let me get you sorted?"

Did he need her cooperation? If so, why? Wasn't he a god? Maybe GMs had limits, too. But regardless of what he'd said about risks in doing what she was doing, she'd rather take those risks than go back to being Sally Streetmonger. She was Sally Adventurer now. Sally Make-Her-Own-Choices.

Well, Sally something or other, anyway. She hadn't yet thought of a new name to suit her new status.

She pointed to something behind the guy. "What's that?"

"What?" He turned.

Sally ran as fast as she could in the direction Darthrok and Essley had gone.

4

_____

THE FUNNY THING about running in a random direction, in an unknown place, with no intended destination, is that it's impossible to get more lost than one already is.

When Sally felt certain she'd lost Somewhat Threatening Guy, she slowed down and observed her surroundings. She'd already gone far from the spot that Darthrok had lost her, and wandering, in her opinion, would neither help nor hurt her. Curious about absolutely everything, she chose to see whatever she could as long as she happened to be there.

She wished she had one of those voice transmitters that allowed for communicating over long distances. Maybe she could find one, and contact her friends that way. She'd have to watch for a place to buy a communicator.

She appeared to be in a little hamlet, or maybe she was just on the outskirts of a town. Pink, yellow, and blue streamers fluttered in the wind, drawing her attention. They'd been attached to a large lattice with a door-sized shape cut out of it.

Why would there be such an opening, fluttering with decoration, if not to invite her to step through?

She planted her pretty leather boot in the dirt and pushed her way in.

A glance over her shoulder satisfied her that Somewhat Threatening Guy hadn't followed her, which gave her the luxury of being able to take in the scene before her.

Balloons.

Balloons everywhere.

A heart-shaped one bonked her in the face, bouncing off her nose with an interesting, hollow sound and rolling several times as it drifted to the ground.

"Sorry!" a little girl called, running up and ducking her head, looking abashed.

Sally smiled. "It's okay. Didn't hurt."

The little girl would be ideal to ask questions of, since she'd be unlikely to become suspicious if Sally said anything really strange. Frustratingly, Sally's words, even the ones she was really good at, had a way of receding away from her when she got excited.

The child retrieved her balloon from the grass and ran off before Sally could wrestle her vocabulary into submission.

A middle-aged man wearing a pale gray suit strolled by, carrying a basket. He paused when he saw her. Smiling, he reached into the basket and plucked out a stick with a star-shaped balloon fixed to the end. He extended it toward her. "Here you go. Enjoy the festival. Be sure to enter the raffle!"

She accepted the stick, delighted that someone would just wander up and give her something without asking for anything in return. "Thank you!"

He tipped his top hat at her and strode onward, whistling.

Gently waving her balloon-stick experimentally, she glanced around to see other people holding them, too. Or wearing them tucked into a backpack. The sticks didn't appear to be good for much besides being festive, but it was her first present, so she liked it.

She wove her way through the area, sometimes following a line of people walking the same direction and sometimes threading her way through little clusters of folks who had collected. Sometimes people looked up and gave her a pleasant smile or tip of a hat, but mostly everyone was involved with whoever they were with.

Festivals were a social event, it seemed.

And here she was, alone.

Well, so what? She might lack companions, a reasonable vocabulary, and the ability to avoid getting distracted by interesting things, but she wouldn't let any of that get in her way.

She stopped for a few minutes to watch a balloon artist twist air-filled tubes into fun shapes. A rabbit. A bicycle. A pineapple.

A young man stood by, wearing an elaborate balloon creation of a black steam train as a hat.

Sally kind of wanted a hat like that.

Browsing the many booths and tents, she found mugs etched with hot air balloons, zeppelin necklaces, and huge solar balloons in the shapes of snakes, caterpillars, and mythical dragons and sea serpents. She admired them, but had no need for a mug.

Not all the items for sale were balloon-related. Moving on, she also noted items like scented soaps and ornate door-knockers. The majority of items, though, seemed to express a fanatical reverence for balloons of all types.

"Enter for a chance to win a ride!" a man called out, indicating a clear box filled with blue tickets.

"On what?" she asked.

His gaze came around quickly, latched onto her, and he smiled. "On a hot air balloon. One lucky winner will get to ride from here to their choice of three local towns."

That sounded fun.

"How much?" she asked. Saying the phrase made her giggle. She'd heard people say that to her many, many thousands of times. Now she was the one asking.

She was getting the hang of this adventuring thing.

"One silver."

Even if she cared about money, that much would be pocket change. She handed him a silver coin and he tore off a ticket, then ripped it in half. "You're number two hundred fifty-eight. Sounds like a lucky one, right?"

He probably said that to everyone. The guy gave a weird vibe that made Sally disinclined to trust him.

Nonetheless, she smiled and nodded. He didn't need to know she didn't trust him. It was enough for her to know.

"Good luck!" He waved at her in a clear dismissal as he turned to a trio of adventurers who apparently wanted to try their luck, too.

As she tucked the ticket into an inner pocket of her dress, a scent in the air made her pause. It reminded her of the churros smell, and if there were churros, or something like them, in her vicinity, she felt it imperative to find them and make them hers.

She followed her nose to one of the more popular tents at the festival, judging by the attention it received. This tent was large, red, and held up by numerous metal poles that anchored heavy tethers. More importantly, the irresistible aroma intensified, drawing her toward it. She smelled something similar to churros, but it was a sweeter smell with some other, undefined scent. She didn't know what it was, but she needed it.

"Fresh batch! Still a bit warm, even," a woman announced.

Sally couldn't see what was on offer because of the people ahead of her, but she rode the wave of people until she stood at the front. Mimicking what she'd observed others doing, she handed over a coin, then received some other coins and a warm paper bag in return.

She heard people saying "caramel corn" repeatedly, so she felt reasonably sure that this what she'd purchased. What that meant, though, she didn't know. She was familiar with the concept of caramel, and that of corn, but how those things had combined to make the thing she held was a mystery to her.

Some puzzles are meant for solving, and some are for eating. Well, not many are meant for eating, but Sally had made up her mind in this specific case.

Once out of the tent, she unfolded the top of the bag and found some lumpy blobs with a firm, golden-brown coating. She picked up one of the blobs and put it in her mouth.

She chewed carefully, closing her eyes in bliss. Why had she always envisioned skinny yellow tubes when people mentioned corn?

She wondered, fleetingly, if adventurers might have cognitive issues. It was okay if they did, but understanding their inner workings would be helpful.

Finding an unoccupied bench, she sat, munching on her treat and hoping to do some people watching.

Her crossbow hung awkwardly, keeping her from raising her arm comfortably. Annoying! She didn't even want to use the thing. Why was she still lugging it around?

She shrugged off her backpack, not sorry to be relieved of its weight for the moment. Then she removed the crossbow and the bolt pouch, putting them on the bench beside her, alongside her balloon stick.

Much better.

She happily ate her caramel corn and watched the festival goers. There were far more adventurers than CMs, and it could be instructive to study their behavior. Finding patterns would help her in her new life as an adventurer.

She froze in mid-chew. Oh!

Adventurers! Essley and Darthrok!

They must be looking for her. She'd been so flustered by Somewhat Threatening Guy then distracted by the festival that she'd failed to consider how her disappearance must have affected them.

Blazing currents! She needed to find them! But...how? What would they have done when they backtracked and couldn't find her?

If they had any sense, they'd go on to Pivot and wait in her shop.

Oh, her shop!

What was she doing, sitting here eating scrumptious caramel corn when she needed to get back to her shop? How had she let the lure of excitement and the unknown steal her focus?

Cursing herself as having scrap for brains, she grabbed her backpack and hurried back toward the way she'd come. Could she make it back to Pivot on her own? Theoretically, she had the tools, if she concentrated on them and didn't get distracted.

"Hey! Hey, miss!" a voice shouted behind her. Then, more urgently, "You, in the fancy pants?"

Sally had fancy pants. No, she had *very* fancy pants. She paused to look back over her shoulder.

She saw a young adventurer waving her crossbow at her.

A woman screamed.

A man shouted.

Suddenly, everyone was screaming and running. A panic was breaking out. Though it was utterly fascinating to see people misinterpreting the situation and losing their minds, Sally didn't have time for this.

Should she go grab the weapon from the fool, so he'd stop freaking people out?

In her moment of indecision, a familiar form shifted into view.

Sally's breath froze in her throat. Kitria.

Her nemesis scanned the chaotic crowd with an expression of bemused interest, then her gaze caught on Sally and doubled back.

Sally saw the flash of recognition and cold terror streaked through her. Kitria would kill her. Kitria always killed her. And Kitria would want to know why Sally was somewhere that she had no business being.

No, no, no, this had all gone so wrong, so fast. Was this normal for adventuring?

Sally bent her knees and rounded her back, losing a good eight inches of height as she slouched. She let her hair swing down in front of her face. She bumped into several people as she hurried away.

A pair of hands grabbed and held her shoulders and she tried to reel backward.

"Sally!" Somewhat Threatening Guy stared into her eyes, his face only an arm's length away. He worried her less than Kitria, so she didn't pull away.

"Pivot!" she cried in desperation. "Pivot, pivot!"

His jaw set and he nodded. Before she could protest, he wrapped her in a tight hug and everything went dark.

SALLY MATERIALIZED IN HER STORE, behind the counter, just as always. An adventurer leaned over to peer inside a cabinet, but straightened when she appeared.

"How can I help you today?" Sally asked with her customary smile.

The adventurer named Mott stepped forward. She was a Southern maker, though she hadn't yet chosen a specialty. "I have a puzzle. Can you help me solve it?"

"Let's have a look!" Sally answered, pleased. She'd expected a request for a cloak or tool or weapon. The opportunity to solve a puzzle was much, much better.

In spite of everything going on in her life, puzzles remained a source of fascination and delight for her.

Mott placed a metal star the size of a pocket watch on the counter. Sally leaned down, studying it. She could flip her goggles down to examine it, to see greater details than her eyes could see on their own, but she preferred to solve puzzles without any help.

"One gold," she said. She wasn't sure, but she guessed that this puzzle would yield some kind of temporary attribute boost.

Mott gave her the gold, and she dropped it into the cash register, enjoying the hisses, clunks, and whirrings the machine made. She'd always loved those sounds.

She picked up the little star-shaped puzzle, feeling its weight in her palm and shifting it to see if the weight redistributed itself. It did. She guessed that the puzzle had some kind of dense liquid inside, like oil. Unusual. Puzzles rarely involved liquid.

Experimentally, she held the star between her thumb and second finger of one hand, and gave it a spin with her other hand. Hm, yes, that did something. She gave it a harder spin and felt the liquid move out into the points of the star, where it stayed.

Tapping the center, she found that it now had no liquid in it. That must mean the points were compartments that had been locked off under centrifugal force.

She flipped her goggles down and switched to the lenses that magnified but did nothing else. Peering close, she could see tiny lines between the points and the center.

Aha!

Sally reached under her sales counter and pulled up a small knife. It was a fairly dull knife, intended more for prying things than anything else. When she held it over the puzzle, Mott grabbed her prize off the counter.

"Ack!" she said. "If you can't solve it, just say so."

Sally indicated the knife. "This *is* the solution. Don't worry."

Looking like she was pretty sure she'd be sorry later, Mott put the puzzle back on the counter.

Gently but firmly, Sally wedged the edge of the dull blade into a crack and gave it a sharp twist. The point fell off. She repeated the process four more times, which reduced the puzzle to a tiny metal pentagon.

Moving her goggles back to her head, where she wore them like a headband, she held the knife out to Mott. "You can do it."

The adventurer held the tool uncertainly, looking from Sally to the puzzle.

Sally pantomimed holding the knife sideways and pressing down on it with her opposite palm.

Looking resigned, Mott did so. The pentagon's brittle metal cracked open, and a thin metal band fell out.

Mott seized it, stared at it intently, then hooted. "A short-duration stamina boost! Nice!"

She slipped the ring onto her finger and left with a spring in her step. She didn't thank Sally or tell her goodbye, but that was no surprise. Adventurers didn't think Sally Streetmonger was a real person.

Once Mott had left, she turned to face the back corner of her shop, where Somewhat Threatening Guy hovered as a specter. She could see him, though no one else could.

She hadn't minded that he'd been back there, watching her. In fact, she was glad to have a chance to prove herself.

"How was that?" she demanded. "Normal enough?"

He sighed. "I must be crazy. I should just restore you."

She studied him for a moment. She felt torn between humoring him and telling him off. On one hand, he seemed to have a power over her that she didn't yet understand, but on the other, she really didn't want to be told what to do. "I'm five."

"You're *not* fine," he enunciated. "I looked at your code. You're running your old code and your new code, at the same time. That shouldn't even be possible."

"I'm fancy," she assured him.

His arms flailed with desperate, but comic frustration. "What does that even mean?"

Sally steeled herself and focused. She imagined the word "five," then replaced the sound of the second consonant with the *n* sound, as she'd done before. It still didn't come naturally, but if she was very careful, she could make it happen.

"I'm fine," she said with great effort.

Okay, the word sounded more like *faaeeenuh* but she'd assembled that word herself, and judging by Guy's face, he understood.

She'd consider it a success.

He frowned. "What happened to you? And you'd better have a good answer, or I'll just restore you to a backup. Seriously. Give me a reason to leave you like this."

She studied his plain-featured, entirely forgettable face. He was so nondescript that she wondered if she'd even recognize him if he left and come back. Nah, she would. No one could possibly be completely unremarkable.

Despite his lack of physical characteristics, though, she had a sense that he *cared* about her. Cared about what happened to her. He *wanted* to be convinced by whatever she said next.

What was it Darthrok had said? Something about how adventurers were really good at seeing what they wanted to see. Maybe this guy was similar to them.

She stepped toward him and put a hand on his arm. She didn't know why, but she sensed that physical contact would mean something to him. "I'm Sally," she said, putting energy into each word, imbuing it with hidden meaning.

She didn't know what that hidden meaning was, but with luck, he would draw out whatever it was he was hoping to find.

His lips pressed together pensively and she added, "I'm a puzzle."

She smiled knowingly at him.

"So..." he said hesitantly, "you've graduated into a new level of adaptive learning? And that's how you're running both types of code? Is that what you're saying?"

His words were nonsense, but she favored him with a look of understanding. "It's guaranteed."

He ran a hand through his hair. "Well, it's strange timing, considering everything that's happening with the company, but I guess it makes sense."

He sighed. "It's too bad this didn't happen sooner."

Sally wondered why he suddenly looked so sad. She didn't know what he really was, but he emanated a sense of regret. She said cheerfully, "I'm doing my best. Don't tell your friends."

A wistful smile twisted his lips and dissipated the regret. "Right. It's our secret. Just like always."

Always? What did that mean? Her inquisitive reflexes screamed at her to ask him questions so she could solve the puzzle of his words, but she restrained herself. A deep instinct told her that expressing interest would shatter her illusion. He'd stop seeing what he wanted to see.

She simply continued to smile.

"Okay," he said. "I'll check in with you soon. Might be a few days. I've been...busy."

She remained passive, sensing that such behavior met his expectations.

He disappeared.

Sally let out a long breath, leaning forward and resting on her shop counter. She didn't know what had happened, but she knew that she had squeaked out of a tight spot.

And only just barely.

And he'd be back soon.

AFTER THE MYSTERIOUS GUY LEFT, Sally's usual trickle of customers became a stream that took her a couple of hours to work through.

She found it all too easy to fall back on her old phrases and behavior patterns. Everything clicked right in, as if she'd never left. A few people noted her clothing change, but the vast majority didn't seem to notice. They only wanted to get money for their scrap metal and parts, or replace damaged tools, or upgrade their items.

To them, she remained nothing. A non-entity that didn't even deserve a "hello" or a "goodbye," much less a "please" or "thank you."

She should be relieved. If they were fooled, it would help keep Somewhat Threatening Guy fooled, too. But the lack of courtesy was like a pebble in Sally's shiny boot, rubbing an injury into her flesh. No, it wasn't a lack of courtesy, exactly. It was the lack of acknowledgement. The failure to treat her as human.

She hated that.

She'd never hated anything before. Not even all those times she'd had a sword run through her. That had been a minor inconvenience.

Being unacknowledged as a person cut much more deeply.

Though her store rarely attracted crowds, at the height of the sudden rush, it was tough for people to get in without bumping into others. Sally efficiently sold and bought, bought and sold, and answered questions about which items would be a better choice. She wasted little time on haggling, which she usually enjoyed. Finally, she reduced the crowd to a pair of adventurers, sold them what they needed, and wished them good adventuring.

"Wonder where she went," a Southern scholar muttered

to her companion after selling a heap of scrap metal to Sally.

"Who cares?" the companion answered. "So long as we got what we needed."

Sally stared after them as they left, leaving her alone. She was still staring at the door when Essley and Darthrok hurried in, looking frantic.

"There you are!" Darthrok exclaimed. "What happened?"

Sally remained impassive for a socially awkward amount of time, then pasted on a bright smile. "Hello! What brings you here today?"

The two froze in place, then exchanged a worried look.

"Sally?" Essley asked cautiously.

"I got some new puzzles in," she confided, just as she would have in the old days.

"Oh no..." Darthrok's face fell. "She's been reset."

They looked too sad and Sally felt like a meanie. She said slyly, "Just fitting, guys."

"Just...what?" Essley's expression cleared. "Hang on. Did you mean, 'just kidding?'"

"It's guaranteed," Sally nodded, giggling.

Their expressions slid from surprised to irritated, then to relieved, and finally settling on outraged.

"You were messing with us?" Darthrok asked, incredulous.

Sally nodded. "Just fitting around."

Essley let out a startled laugh. "Well, you did kind of the same thing with her when you gave her that device. I guess she's paying you back."

Darthrok's mouth opened, but no words came out. He looked from Essley to Sally and back again.

"Payback," Sally agreed. She already knew both of those

words, and putting them together was just a matter of saying them quickly.

Was she getting better at making new things to say? She hoped so.

"Wow," Darthrok said, rolling his shoulders as if to release tension. "Okay, I guess that's fair. But what the doot! We were really worried! What happened?"

She pressed her lips together, searching for a way to explain it. She didn't have all the words she needed, so she'd have to do her best to get the ideas across. "My condition is good. Someone got me and I stopped. Then, a big thing with people. Then Kitria, and I ran. The someone person brought me here."

"Oh man, you ran into Kitria?" Essley stepped closer to the counter and rested her hands on it. "And somebody helped you get away? Helped you get back here?"

Sally nodded. The fact that Somewhat Threatening Guy had seemed somewhat threatening went unsaid because the words to describe him eluded her. Nor could she explain how he'd gotten her here. Not only did she lack the words, but she didn't understand what had happened.

"I'm glad you made it back, then," Darthrok said. "What then? How was the shop?"

"Lots of people," Sally answered.

"Did anyone notice anything different about you?" Essley asked.

Sally shook her head. "All the same. They take, they go."

"Did no one even notice your clothes?" Essley asked in surprise.

Sally shrugged. "Barely."

"Wait," Darthrok said, looking at her closely. "Where's your crossbow?"

Right. She'd left that behind at the festival, along with her balloon stick. At least she'd grabbed her backpack.

Sally waved a hand dismissively. "Easy come, easy go."

They watched her silently for a few long moments. Essley said, "Well, I guess we aren't going to get more specific details right now. At least you're well. Did Kitria recognize you? No one else has known you, besides the banker."

Sally thought back to that moment when her gaze crossed Kitria's. She'd definitely seen a flash of recognition, she was sure of that. But it was only a flash, and she'd moved fast. Maybe Kitria had done a double-take, then decided there was no way she'd seen what she'd thought she'd glimpsed.

The idea that Sally had been gallivanting about a festival should have seemed ridiculous to Kitria. Hopefully she'd laughed off the silly thought and continued with whatever jerk thing she'd been doing at the time.

Was it unfair of her to characterize Kitria as a jerk?

Sally had heard her say that killing Sally on a regular basis wasn't just for fun, it was part of her maintaining her karma as a chaotic neutral person. Kitria hadn't invented the world or its workings. Perhaps it was unfair to use her necessary self-maintenance against her.

On the other hand...Kitria had chosen her alignment and her profession. Nobody had forced her become a thug. And she could surely maintain her karma in some way that didn't mean stabbing Sally to death. That was a purposeful choice she'd made. Repeatedly.

Though she'd mostly considered the deaths a mere inconvenience before, Sally felt much more strongly about them now. She felt angry about it. And when she'd seen Kitria, she'd felt fear, and that made her mad, too.

Yes, indeed, Kitria could rightfully be called a jerk.

Jerk, jerk, jerk. A steamin' heck of a jerk.

Sally noticed Essley and Darthrok staring at her with concern. Right. She'd gotten distracted by her thoughts and been silent for too long again.

If only she could expose her thoughts to them, instead of having to keep them inside. She needed more words. Somewhat Threatening Guy had suggested something about that. If she ever saw him again, which she mostly hoped she didn't, she'd have to ask him about expanding her vocabulary.

"I'm fine," she said in response to the question about whether anyone had recognized her. This time, the word *fine* came out sounding almost natural. Nice! "Fancy. No one sees Sally."

"Good," Essley said. "That might complicate things. At least for now, it's good to stay incognito."

"So what's it like being back here?" Darthrok asked. "After seeing a bit of the world outside, is it uncomfortable to be back here again?"

"No," she answered thoughtfully. "The condition here is good. Helping is good. I like it here." She paused, thinking hard on how to express her next thought. "Others who aren't you can be bad."

Essley pursed her lips. "You're saying that other adventurers treat you poorly?"

"Some," Sally agreed. "Most just ignore. But I'm of good quality. I want to be valued."

"Well, at least we know you're special," Darthrok said. "It's a start, right?"

Sally considered, then nodded. "Yes. Something started. I can't waste it."

Darthrok raised his fist as if to hit her and she took a

step back before she realized he wasn't threatening her. He held his fist out, as if offering her to take it. She looked to Essley for help.

Essley made two fists, then bumped her right against her left.

Ah. Sally curled her fingers into a fist and bumped it against Darthrok's. She suspected that this was some kind of ritual from their homeland. Her suspicion seemed confirmed when Darthrok cheered.

"Yeah!" he exclaimed. "We'll take it as far as it goes."

Essley nodded.

The pair didn't know what "as far as it goes" might mean, but in truth, neither did Sally. They'd have to find out together.

5

SALLY REMAINED in her store for the next two hours, serving customers just as she always had, while Essley and Darthrok went off to run some personal errands.

Well, not *just* as she always had. In between customers, she explored her home with new eyes. Everything looked the same, but with much greater resolution, as if she'd gotten some new goggle lenses that improved her regular sight by a thousand times.

It wasn't at all like a prison, as Darthrok had suggested. The wood planks that made up the floor, ceiling, and walls had a polished shine and a lovely grain pattern. Her sales counter had a granite top with a yellowy-beige pattern that had sparkly flecks here and there. The cabinets holding her wares were neatly organized and well-stocked with goods. Sally had always liked to imagine that her products had eager energy—that they couldn't wait to get out into the world and start doing what they were meant to do.

Had she been reflecting her own hidden desires on them?

She had a beautiful old cash register too, which had

been restored and updated over the decades, making it a gorgeous paradox of modern anachronism. Tracing a finger over the number keys, she thanked it for its years of stead-fast service.

She liked her home. She really did. But that didn't mean she wanted to be confined here. She'd received word that the town would be moving in an hour, and after they'd settled in the new spot, she intended to do some exploring. She needed to come up with a solution for knowing when customers arrived while she was out, though. She didn't want to inconvenience people, or cause a stir that would get Somewhat Threatening Guy's attention.

The world awaited her, and she couldn't wait to get back out and see what else she could find.

Opening her cabinets, she began grabbing things and putting them on the counter. She had only a vague idea of what she wanted to do, and hoped that her inventory would help her figure out the rest as she went.

———

ESSLEY RETURNED to Sally's store first, shortly before Pivot began its shift to a new location. She approached the counter with a curious expression. "What's that?"

Sally frowned at the collection of items she'd assembled. Try as she might, she couldn't get them properly aligned.

She pointed to the door. "For that. My store can't be poor."

Essley looked from the metal-cutter in Sally's hand to the assembly of parts. "Is it...some kind of doorbell?"

Sally wasn't sure about that. "It's to know if customers are here. Because I forget about things."

"So it is a doorbell."

"Okay," Sally agreed. "But it doesn't work."

"Why not?" Essley reached out a hand to touch the device, then pulled it back as if she had second thoughts about doing so.

Sally gave her a peeved look.

Essley let out a short laugh. "Right. You don't know why it won't work. I'm no help, though. I've got zero mechanical know-how. Kind of sad, right? Sometimes I wish I'd ignored everyone's advice that a Northerner should be a mercenary. Sure, I heal fast and don't get hurt as easily, but hitting stuff all the time gets boring, you know?"

"So change," Sally said absently, trying to figure out why she couldn't get the cogs of two gears to line up properly. Every time she tried, they worked briefly, then the timing went wrong and the gears ground to a stop.

It was seriously vexing.

Essley stood up straighter. "What, you mean retrain? That'd be so much work."

"So?" Sally asked, picking up a socket wrench to tighten a bolt on the other side of her device. Maybe the metal pieces she'd used weren't pressed together tightly enough, and was allowing the metal to shift slightly when the pieces were moving.

"*So*, I'd have to start over in a new guild. I'd have to either give up all my mercenary skills and start fresh with the ones from a new profession. Or else, freeze all my merc skills and learn new skills at half-speed. It would be a long time before I could get back to where I am now."

Sally stopped fiddling with her creation to focus entirely on Essley. Right now, her friend's misaligned parts seemed more important. "What profession would you want?"

"Well, I've been working up to being a bodyguard, so I can help good people. You know, protect them from the mean mercenaries. I thought it would be cool to kind of be a rogue of my own kind. But in truth, it stinks because other mercenaries think I'm a goody-goody, and non-mercs dislike mercs. Because, you know, they tend to be jerks. So, basically, I'm disliked on both sides and to be honest, some days it really just stinks."

She heaved out a heavy breath, then continued her line of thought. "But if I were going to choose a different profession, knowing what I know now of Everternia, I'd like to be a maker. A botanist, I think. Then I could make medicines and potions. And, heck, since botanists usually work with doctors, maybe I'd meet someone, you know, special."

It seemed obvious to Sally that whether Essley changed professions or not, she'd meet new people on a daily basis. Maybe she meant she'd meet someone who didn't treat her poorly for being a merc. Sally knew how it felt to be something that people treated like bog slime, so a change of profession seemed like the best option for Essley.

"You can stay the same and be not fancy," Sally said slowly, trying to find the best words in her vocabulary to convey her thoughts. "Or you can change and be what you want."

Essley picked absently at a button on her jacket. "So you're saying I can continue being less than satisfied, or do the hard work to reach for something better. Right?"

Sally nodded.

Essley nodded. "Yeah. I think you might be right. I'll think about it. But after Pivot moves, I think I know how we can make your doorbell work."

Sally smiled. "Is that right?"

"Yeah, pretty sure. Or if not, we could figure out a different solution. There are lots of ways to do something. We only have to find *one* of them."

Darthrok came hurrying in, carrying a small package. "Whew! Made it. I was at the bank when they said we had five minutes until Pivot shifts. So, how do Essley and I know how to meet up with you once you arrive at the new spot?"

Sally had already thought about that. She reached out and touched both Essley's and Darthrok's hands, forming a group that she was now leader of.

Wow. She was a leader. She'd never been one before, but she felt incredibly good about it. Strong. Reliable. "Like this. Just stay."

"We won't get kicked out?" Darthrok looked skeptical.

"Not sure," Sally said. "But I think this will work. I can't leave during a shift."

He said, "So...if you're coded to remain here during the shift—which makes sense, because you're supposed to be the one driving the store—you think Essley and I being grouped to you will keep us from getting booted out when the shift starts?"

Essley smiled. "It makes sense that it might work that way. Good thinking, Sally."

Sally smiled back, pleased with the praise. "Let's go."

"Go where?" Darthrok asked.

Sally brought her hands up to chin level and pantomimed shifting a lever, then holding a wheel and driving.

"Ohhh, wow, you actually drive? I always thought that was kind of a hidden mechanic that we just had to imagine."

Sally tried to make sense of his words, then dismissed them. He said strange things sometimes. Probably because he came from very far away, and didn't always know how things really worked here.

It was kind of cute, how naïve they were about such things.

IN THE COCKPIT of Sally's store, Essley and Darthrok looked around with the curiosity of children while Sally focused on the coordinates she'd received.

Watching through the opened window, she monitored her instruments, which gave her constant readouts of her current coordinates and her shop's attitude in relation to the two planes.

Her companions had been briefly amazed when she'd opened the window in the side of her store, revealing everything that lay ahead. When closed, that spot didn't look like a window at all. Since adventurers were forced to track Pivot down wherever it went to cultivate their basic skills, the town had measures for making sure it couldn't be followed.

Therefore, the idea that Pivot's buildings had openings in them had struck Essley and Darthrok as kind of amazing.

It was cute how little they knew about the world they lived in.

At first, Sally had considered them so much more worldly than herself, but the more she observed, the more she realized that it wasn't true. Yes, they had far more experience in many areas, but she apparently knew things intrinsic to Everternia that they'd never even considered.

How had they *thought* Pivot traveled from place to place? That it magically appeared and disappeared? Silly adventurers!

The move was neither particularly long nor particularly short. As far as Pivot's shifts went, it was entirely average, which meant that it took long enough for Essley and Darthrok to get bored. Their excitement over the novelty faded quickly. When they finally arrived at the new location, the pair was eager to get out and go do something.

She'd given them the coordinates of the new spot, but the description had meant nothing to them. They'd just have to take a look to see what it was like.

Upon arrival, Sally oriented her store as she'd been directed, then disengaged the engine, making sure all its parts ceased activity, vented steam, and began to cool. Then the three went back to the storeroom.

"What's this on the counter, Sally?" Darthrok asked on the way. "I noticed it on the way in. Did someone sell it to you?"

Sally shook her head. She went to the item in question and put her hand on it possessively. "I made it. It isn't fancy yet. Essley said she could help."

Darthrok shot Essley a dubious look. "You, help with something mechanical? I don't think so."

"Not me," Essley shook her head in exasperation. "But there *is* someone in this town who's a master technie. Remember?"

"Oh, right. Let's do that, then." Darthrok looked to Sally. "Do you want me to carry it for you?"

She didn't really want to put it in a container and jostle it around, but she did need help to complete it. "No, thank you. I'll take it."

She bent down and reached beneath the counter, pulling out a black box used for gifting. It was the sturdiest container she had. Carefully, she put her invention into it and covered it with the lid, then put the box into a shoulder bag.

She followed Essley and Darthrok out into the newly-settled town of Pivot, hoping that whoever they were taking her to would provide the help she needed.

Already, people hurried by, though rather than the customary streams of people, Sally saw a mere trickle.

Interesting. She'd never really thought about what happened to the town's flow of traffic after a shift. Her store's traffic flow was so entirely sporadic and unpredictable that she'd assumed it was just a function of how the town worked. Later, when she had some quiet moments, she intended to reflect on her burgeoning views on Pivot's realities in relation to her previous assumptions.

Maybe the things she'd taken for granted in the past actually had much deeper meanings.

When Essley approached a door Sally had seen once before, Sally paused. "You said no before."

She'd been attracted to the stout but somehow also sleek store, with its sharp edges and smooth seams. Something about it suggested a more sophisticated type of fabrication than any other place in Pivot. This was Sujan's store, and he was a highly acclaimed master technie.

A quiver of excitement ran through Sally. She didn't know what to expect, but the place seemed wonderfully grand to her nonetheless. Like a cave of wonders or a treasure trove.

"That was when we didn't have an appointment," Essley said. "I made one when I first saw your invention. Somehow, I figured one way or another, you and Sujan needed to meet."

The mercenary looked extremely pleased with herself.

"You're sure?" Darthrok paused with his hand raised to ring the doorbell, giving Essley a dubious look. "You know how he can be."

"How can he be?" Sally asked.

Essley made a dismissive gesture. "He's not that bad, when you understand him. Besides, if anyone can handle him, Sally can." She shifted her gaze to Sally. "Don't worry. It'll be fine."

Sally hoped that was true.

Essley rang the bell, and when the door made a loud click, she opened it. Darthrok followed. Sally hung back for a moment, just in case they got thrown out on their ears by the notoriously inflexible technie. When they didn't, she cautiously stepped in behind them.

Once inside, she froze. A feeling of wonder seized her innards and then seeped all the way out to her fingers and toes.

Sujan's shop was *amazing*. There were multiple worktables and neat stacks of storage bins, as well as rails screwed into the wall. Each worktable was carefully arranged, either with an empty surface or with a few things sitting at right angles to one another.

It was as if precise, mechanical angels had arranged everything here. The storage bins were all of the same size, perfectly positioned, and lidded so that they gave no hint about their contents. The hanging rails gave Sally more to view as they anchored hooks that held a variety of tools, all hung up shortest to longest.

Impeccably organized.

Though the care that had been put into the layout and upkeep was impressive on its own, what really set Sally's insides on fire was the feeling of purpose.

Every item in Sujan's workshop, she was certain, was here for a reason and would never go forgotten or neglected. And what things he must create in such a place! What wonders he must repair!

Whatever problem she might ever encounter, surely, this place contained a solution.

She even loved the smell. Metallic and a little burned with a hint of freshly-cut wood.

A clipped, distinctly Eastern-sounding voice broke into

Sally's reverie. "If you aren't going to close the door, kindly take two steps back so I can."

Sally looked behind her. Two steps back would put her on the doorstep outside the shop. If she did that and he closed the door, he'd be slamming it right in her face—*oh.*

Right. Sujan was irritable, and he'd just told her off before she could even greet him.

But she was Sally Streetmonger, not some nervous adventurer. If he thought a few rude words would chase her away, he was in for a surprise.

She closed the door and strode forward, extending her hand to him. "I'm Sally. Good to meet you."

He looked at her hand with disdain. "What's that for?"

"A greeting that's customary for my people. You'd be rude to refuse." She smiled at him pleasantly, noticing for the first time that he was probably the most handsome man she'd ever seen.

Gorgeous, really.

He arched an eyebrow. It made him look arrogant, but somehow no less good-looking. "I don't touch people I don't know."

The cold disdain in his voice, for some perverse reason, only made Sally's smile widen. She'd always been courteous, even when someone stabbed her to death. But today, some wild seed of naughtiness suddenly made her want to vex this dismissive man.

"Well, you know me now. Sally. Remember it." She snapped her fingers with an elaborate flourish.

She justified her wicked impulse to herself, reasoning that since karma was a measurable phenomenon in Everternia, surely Sujan had some payback due to him, and why shouldn't Sally be the one to deliver it?

As far as she was concerned, the math worked.

Essley and Darthrok, however, stood gaping at her as if she'd lost her mind. She gave them a sunny smile.

Turning back to Sujan, she assessed him.

Sujan Souk, CM.

Class: Maker.

Specialty: Technie.

He had no money on him at the moment, and he looked like he'd give her a good fight.

Hmm. He clearly didn't recognize her. No CMs had, thus far.

She wondered about his fighting skill. He seemed about as formidable as her, and both of them were supposedly capable of pounding Essley and Darthrok into the dirt, even though Sally had no weapons skills and no combat experience.

That, in itself, was a puzzle.

"Your shop is beautiful," she told him.

He blinked. Whatever he'd expected her to say, that hadn't been it. He recovered quickly. "Since you made an appointment, I assume you came here for more than sightseeing."

She smiled. "Indeed. I'd like your expertise." She gestured to her bag, then to an empty worktable. "May I?"

He made a half-hearted gesture of permission.

Carefully, she set the gifting box on the table and removed her door alert mechanism, arranging it so he could see her intentions. "I got this far, then I got stuck."

Sujan moved closer, looking like he was curious in spite of himself and trying not to show it. "It's interesting. I haven't seen an adventurer try to do something like this. It's an alarm system, right? For security?"

"More like, just a long-distance doorbell," she said. "And I'm not—" She almost told him she wasn't an adventurer.

Why? She might be a CM, too, but she had earned the right to call herself an adventurer. Why had she been tempted to tell him her secret?

She needed to be more careful. She nearly made a serious mistake.

"I'm not skilled enough to finish it," she finished smoothly to cover her misspeak.

"It's not terrible work for a mid-level technie," he mused as he picked up one of the smaller pieces. "But this material isn't compatible with the rest. Either you need to switch this out to something we can forge-weld, or we can change out all the rest and join it with a laser torch."

"I can't fasten the two together?" she asked, leaning closer to examine the piece he held. "Like with bolts or something?"

"You could, but the other metal will wear because it's softer, and the two parts will end up walking away from each other, causing your fasteners to break. Then the whole contraption is likely to get destroyed, if it's working at the time. A wrench in the works, as we like to say."

She made a humming sound of understanding. It was just as well she hadn't been able to get those pieces to fit together right.

But wait. He'd called her a mid-level technie.

"What do you see when you look at me?" she asked.

He pulled his attention from their work to look at her, startled. Sally realized how close their faces were and pulled back just a little, trying to be subtle about it.

"What?" he asked.

"Assess me, please," she said.

Frowning in puzzlement, he gazed at her intently. "Sally. Hidden class. Hidden specialty. You look like you'd be a good match in a fight."

He shrugged.

"Hidden class and specialty? Have you seen that before?" she asked.

"I don't recall." He returned his attention to the device. "I can complete this for you in two days. It will cost you six gold. Do you accept?"

He'd slipped back into his canned responses. Sally felt like she'd been slapped. Speaking to him was much easier than trying to speak to Essley and Darthrok. When she talked to Sujan, words just fell together in the right ways, without her even having to try.

She'd felt like they were having a real conversation, when in reality, he was just going through one of his interaction loops.

The realization stung her.

"I accept," she agreed flatly. She palmed her coins, then deliberately reached toward him and pressed them into his palm. She touched his hand with both of hers and watched him, hoping the contact would cause him to wake up, just like she had.

She held her breath, hoping.

His hand closed around the coins and he pulled away. "Let's keep this professional, miss."

Sally winced. She shouldn't feel hurt. She shouldn't.

So why did she?

Inspiration struck her. "But I don't want you to do the work," she said.

He blinked at her. "I don't understand."

"I'm a technie," she said, and while that hadn't been true when she'd walked in, it was now. Officially, anyway. She logged her new class and specialty right then and there, officially, and she felt a sensation like a dozen doors within her mind suddenly flying open.

Wow!

"Assess me," she told him.

"Sally, what are you doing?" Essley asked.

Sally held up a staying hand and sent Essley a pleading look. She'd explain later, or at least try to.

Rather than complain about having already assessed her, Sujan did so. "Sally. Class: maker. Specialty: technie. You look like you'd give me a good fight. You are not yet apprenticed to anyone."

"Not apprenticed?" Sally looked at Essley and Darthrok. "How do I choose a mentor?"

They shrugged. Darthrok said, "We're the wrong class to ask that. Entrepreneurs have class, specialty, and subspecialty rather than doing an apprenticeship like makers and scholars do."

Right. She knew that. Sometimes her energy got ahead of her knowledge.

"I choose you as my mentor," she said to Sujan.

His eyes lit up and for the first time since she'd entered his shop, his mouth turned up in a smile. Wow, he was even more beautiful when he was happy.

He laughed.

"Your work is acceptable, but unremarkable," he said. "You have to prove yourself worthy of my teaching."

Ouch. Sally grimaced. Then she realized that he had just said that her work was unremarkable for the mid-level technie he believed her to be.

Sally grinned, realizing she was legitimately a mid-level technie. How was that even possible? She was ahead of things already. "Right. I'll be back in two days, then."

With another quick look around at the place she intended to see a lot of in the near future, she led the way out of the shop.

"What was that about, Sally?" Darthrok asked. "You looked like a whipped puppy one second, then grinned like a fiend the next."

Essley focused on the other matter. "You decided to be a technie? Wow! Congratulations!"

Essley wrapped Sally in a big hug.

"Uh, yeah," Darthrok said. "That, too. Congratulations."

He smiled and put his fist up. Remembering the gesture from before, she bumped her own fist against his, feeling quite pleased with herself for learning their sometimes-odd ways.

"I have a new plan," she said, beginning the walk back to her own store. Until she had the alert set up, she didn't feel comfortable leaving it for very long.

"What's the plan?" Essley asked.

"Become Sujan's apprentice."

6

"Wow, your first quest!" Essley chirped as they arrived back at Sally's shop. No adventurers stood waiting for her, and Sally didn't have the sense of doom of having impatient customers that she'd had before.

That was good, but it would be much better when she had the notification system installed so she'd have a constant awareness of what was going on in her shop. She had become an adventurer, and a technie too, but she was still dedicated to the idea of serving her customers well.

She wasn't sure how she'd balance her development as both an adventurer and a technie, but she felt certain she'd discover the solution to that particular puzzle.

She'd keep trying until she figured it out.

"First quest," Sally agreed, satisfied. Out of habit, she grabbed a cloth and began wiping her already-spotless sales counter. When she realized what she was doing, she dropped the cloth, dismayed.

Apparently, her old subroutines were still active. She'd have to stay mindful of that. She didn't want to behave like an automaton. She made her own choices now.

She paused to splice some words together. As soon as she'd left Sujan's shop, she'd returned to finding speech somewhat difficult. "Did you have a quest to become mercenaries?"

Hah. Perfect grammar. Nailed it.

Darthrok shook his head. "Nah, it's different for us. Our quest is basically showing up at a thieves' den, declaring our intentions, and getting beaten to death. So, we have to be prepared with a godsend, and when we regenerate, we run back to the spot where we died, where we're accepted as one of them."

Sally shivered. That sounded terrible! She much preferred the quest method. The idea of dying repulsed her.

She didn't even know if she was capable of earning godsends, since she wasn't like other adventurers. She'd probably need to try, at some point, but she hoped she'd never need to use one. Not only did dying seem abhorrent, but she wasn't sure what would happen if it occurred.

She feared that she'd go back to how she used to be, and for her, that was the worst thing that could possibly happen.

"What do you think you need to do?" Essley asked.

"I don't know," Sally answered cheerfully. "I'll books more."

"Books?" Essley gave her a curious smile.

"Books!" Sally rushed down to her store's control room, then back. She carefully put the three books she'd taken from the abandoned factory on her shop counter.

"Books!" she repeated.

Darthrok came closer and read the titles. "*Mechanical Theory, Practical Electricity, Supply Chain Management Essentials*. Where did you get these?"

Words failed Sally. She struggled, but none of the relevant terms bubbled to the top of her thoughts. "When we...went..."

Frustrated, she sent a desperate look to Essley.

"The factory?" Darthrok asked.

Sally pointed at him. "Yes! That!"

Why was it so hard to talk to her friends, but effortless to talk to Sujan? It also seemed that the more enthusiastic she felt, the more elusive her words became.

"I wondered if you'd grabbed something." Essley sent Sally a sly smile before flipping *Mechanical Theory* open and scanning a page. "Wow. This is some dry stuff. Did you read this, Sally?"

Dry? Did the pages seem brittle? They'd seemed to be in good shape to Sally. "Yes! Good book!" She felt like an idiot saying such basic words. No, not an idiot. An infant. So for sophistication, she added, "*Very* good book."

Darthrok edged closer, peering over Essley's shoulders. "Wow. Okay, well it's not my thing, but I'm glad you like it. I guess that's how you learned enough to make your door notification device?"

Sally nodded. "I learned a lot."

Oh, wait, that was a whole, normal sentence. Cool.

"You're a woman of unknown talents, Sally Streetmonger," he said as he stepped away from the book, as if relieved of some giant burden.

"Hang on," Essley said. "Is Streetmonger even her name anymore? I don't see it when I look at her."

They both fastened their gazes on her, leaving Sally feeling a little weirded out by the excessive attention.

"You're right, it's gone," Darthrok said. "And Sujan didn't mention it either. He just saw her as 'Sally.'"

"Oh, that's right," Essley said. "What do you think, Sally? Are you still Sally Streetmonger?"

Sally furrowed her brow, focusing her attention inward. She'd always been Sally Streetmonger. If others no longer saw her as that, did that mean she still was?

No. Never mind how others saw her. Did she *feel* like Sally Streetmonger?

Yes.

And no.

She was still what she had been before, but she was more. Better. Smarter. Stronger.

"What do you want us to call you?" Essley asked.

Want. What she wanted mattered now. It mattered more than anything, didn't it? Everything she'd done, from the moment she'd stepped out of her shop and viewed the sky for the first time, had happened because it was her choice. She wanted to be the person who chose. She wanted to be *that* kind of strong.

"Sally...Strong," she said. "I'm Sally Strong." Then, to everyone's great surprise, but most of all her own, she burst into tears.

INTERESTINGLY, it was Darthrok who patted Sally's shoulders while she had a brief, violent cry.

She hadn't even known she *could* cry. Another first. All these new feelings went to such extremes. She wished she had a handbook to navigate it all.

She felt entirely overwhelmed, but also, somehow simultaneously amazing.

Feelings were weird.

Darthrok handed her a wadded-up piece of some kind of cloth that, by Sally's estimation, was fairly clean and worth exactly one copper. She accepted it and dabbed at her cheeks.

"You okay?" he asked.

"I'm okay," she said. Her voice had a strange waver in it that she'd never heard before.

He rubbed her shoulders and patted her back. "That's your first cry, right? Did you get extra experience or anything?"

Sally searched her internal fixings. Though she had experience levels, she couldn't read them. She could only tell when something was in her learning pool and causing her stats to actively rise. Not that she needed to be able to see that. Since learning so much from the books, she could *feel* when her learning pools were filling. If she read too much in one sitting, her senses swam with the overabundance of information and she'd have to wait a while before adding more.

"No experience," she said, irritated. Surely, she should have earned some kind of new skill or something.

Essley and Darthrok laughed, and she realized he'd been joking again.

She smiled at him. She was starting to like his humor. She giggled.

"There you go," he said, giving her a final pat and stepping back. "There's our Sally Strong. You can cry whenever you want to. We'll be right here."

Sally steeled herself and focused on her words. "I'm fine."

Woohoo! That had sounded natural!

"Anyway," Essley said, smiling, "what about your quest? You think reading and learning will do it? You intend to drop a bunch of knowledge on Sujan to impress him?"

Put that way, it did seem a little weak. Sally frowned, thinking. "I'll do something. We'll see."

"Winging it has gotten you this far," Essley said. "Might as well keep going with it."

"Don't fix what isn't broken," Darthrok said. His tone indicated that he agreed with Essley, but Sally didn't grasp his meaning. She tucked the phrase away for future investigation.

She knew what "winging it" meant though, and that wasn't what she was doing. "Winging it" meant having no plan. Sally had a plan. Or at least, she was devising one as she went, and adjusting it every time she gained new information.

She just had a lot to learn before she could uncover *all* the information she would ultimately need. She was only just beginning to learn about Everternia, so she had a lot to catch up on.

She was doing her best. She hoped finding the key to getting Sujan to accept her as an apprentice wasn't too difficult.

TWO DAYS of studying her books made Sally feel smarter, but brought her no closer to impressing Sujan.

Keeping her books behind the counter and studying between customers turned out to be remarkably easy to do. The new location of the town had proved to be more arduous for travelers to reach, and the number of visitors diminished. Only those with an immediate need came to Pivot. The others were either waiting until the town shifted again or getting what they needed from another town.

Of course, new adventurers had no choice but to find Pivot. It was their first goal, and the only way to begin. As a result, Sally's customers during this time were mostly young, somewhat peeved travelers with basic needs.

"There you go." She handed a basic knife and a metal cutter to a freshly-minted mercenary. Having a newfound sympathy for how it felt to start out, Sally would have given the tools away for free if she could. She couldn't do that, though. She had to get coin in exchange for goods in order to make the transaction work.

"Wow, these are pretty good for only five copper. Thanks, Sally!"

Sally smiled at the mercenary. Newbies often used her name for their first visit or two. When they realized it made no difference, they'd quit doing that. But it was nice to be acknowledged, for the moment.

She said, "My best price for you. Don't tell your friends."

"Okay." The happy customer hurried out, toward whatever adventure came next.

Sally checked her pocket watch. Time to go to Sujan's. Darthrok had said he'd go with her if he could, but he must not have made it back to Pivot in time. He'd run off to do some hunting.

Essley had said she'd be sleeping, and apologized in advance for not being able to come. Sally thought it odd to sleep in the middle of the day, but who was she to judge? She hardly ever needed to sleep.

Sally's second time entering Sujan's shop was just as thrilling as the first. Maybe even more so because she was excited to receive her alert system and to try to earn an apprenticeship.

He sat at a workbench, absorbed in looking at a tiny device. He straightened and pushed his goggles up on his head when she entered. "Ah, yes. Your order is ready."

He stood up gracefully and strode over to a storage bin.

He reached in, extracted a box, then brought it to Sally. "Have a good day."

He was dismissing her before she'd even said a word? No way.

"Can you demonstrate it for me?" she asked.

Halfway back to the table and whatever had been occupying his attention before, he stopped and turned with a sigh. "Very well."

He took the box from her, set it on an empty table, and laid its contents out. "The device installs on the door jamb in two parts. One piece on the frame and the other on the door itself. When the door opens, it will log the person who enters, and hold that name until the person leaves again."

He picked up a small, flat disc about the size of a fingernail and handed it to her. "The device will transmit the information to this. As long as this device is on your person, you'll be able to access the information. You'll see that someone has entered, or exited, and who's currently inside. You can adjust the options to give you notifications of all, some, or none of these events. That's it. Questions?"

She looked at the tiny disc pinched between her thumb and index finger. "This seems like it would be easy to lose. Can I make it into something I can wear? Like a necklace or something?"

He shrugged. "As long as you don't puncture the device, it can be altered however you choose."

She nodded.

"Very well. Have a good day."

"Hang on," she said, exasperated. "Why are you in such a hurry to get rid of me?"

"I have work to do," he answered tersely.

"Don't we all?" she muttered. "I've been studying almost

nonstop since I was last here. Do you want to test my knowledge?"

"Why would I do that?" He squinted at her.

"For the apprenticeship."

He gave her a withering stare. "No. Anyone can memorize books. If you want to learn from me, you have to prove your worth."

"So, what, practical application, then?"

He said nothing.

"Fine. I'm supposed to figure it out myself." She blinked. "Hey, I just said 'fine' and it was easy. I had to try so hard to say it before. Do you find me easier to talk to than most people?"

His expression became flat and distant. He didn't know what she was talking about. Although she felt like her ability to speak blossomed in his presence, he apparently found her no more comprehensible than any other adventurer.

She sighed. "Right. I'll go install this and try to figure out how to impress you."

"Good day," he said.

She was getting tired of hearing him say that. Clearly, he said it to people he wanted to get rid of. But she had no intention of letting him shoo her out so easily.

After carefully putting her alert system into the box, she considered the little disc. She'd have to think of a way to wear it, to keep it from getting lost. For the moment, she tucked it into a tiny inside pocket at the waist of her pants. Intended to keep coins safe, it would do a decent job of carrying this, too.

She lifted the box, which was surprisingly heavy, and glanced over at Sujan. He'd returned to leaning over the tiny device on the table, peering at it through his goggles as he shifted the lenses.

Wondering what the thing was, and what he was looking for, she set the box down and went to peer over his shoulder. It was a pocket watch, or at least some tiny version of one. She'd never seen anything like it.

"Quartz movement, atomically synced. Wow." She hadn't meant to speak. Somehow, around him, words just seemed to fall out of her mouth.

Sujan froze for a moment, then his head turned very slightly her way. "How do you know that? You don't even have goggles on."

She pointed, but given the size of the object, it was a useless gesture. She let her hand drop. "It's all right there. Crown, mainspring, the storage of potential energy. Then, the sync to Everternia's world clock."

He pushed his goggles up on his head and turned to stare at her directly.

She stared right back. His scrutiny didn't bother her, but she did notice at these close quarters how unusually beautiful he was. Even the little dark, flat mole just behind his right ear was cute.

Too bad he was rude, and not awake like her.

"What else?" he asked.

She pursed her lips in thought. There was a lot she could say about the device in question, but she had a feeling he sought a particular answer. What facet of this brilliant little creation would *he* find most noteworthy?

"There." She pointed to the device that doubled as both an energy source and a heat sink. "You're drawing on an adventurer's fatigue to power it, while shunting heat energy back into the adventurer's pool to cool the device. It creates a null draw on the person overall, while giving the device perpetual energy. It's brilliant."

Words tumbled out of her mouth just the way she thought them, which felt incredible.

"You can see that?" he sounded more than surprised. More like dumbfounded.

Was he kidding? It was all right there in front of them. Sure, the components were teensy, but they were unmistakable all the same.

She extended a finger and gently poked the mole behind his ear. "As plainly as I can see this. Being small doesn't make something less obvious."

He turned to look at her. For an instant, he seemed as puzzled by her ability to touch him as Sally was. But she was probably just imagining it. He didn't know that he was the only CM she'd ever been able to make physical contact with.

"Well." He straightened. "You're observant."

She grinned. "Observant enough to be your apprentice?"

He gave her a withering stare. "I have high standards. I doubt you'll be able to meet them. Now, kindly be on your way. I have work to do."

Only slightly deflated, Sally went to collect the box she'd set down. Picking it up also lifted her spirits right back up again. She had a neat new mechanism that would allow her to adventure more freely, and she'd impressed Sujan, albeit briefly. She was on the right track with him, surely.

"Okay. I'll check back in soon. I'm going to be your apprentice. Count on it!"

She hurried out to install her new alert notification system.

7

"Okay." Darthrok had admired Sally's store upgrade, and listened to a long explanation of how it worked. "So now that you can receive instant notifications about your shop while you're gone, what do you want to do next?"

Judging from Darthrok's expression, he didn't enjoy hearing all the details behind clever engineering. Though Sally didn't always pick up on things like that, she was getting better at it.

"I want to meet all the CMs," Sally answered.

Darthrok made a strange coughing sound. "All of them?"

"The ones in Pivot, to start," she said.

"Okay, that's not too tough. I thought you meant all the CMs in all the cities."

"Eventually." Sally nodded. "But for now, Pivot."

"Okay, but why?" he asked.

She had known he'd ask that, and she felt triumphant that he'd proven her right. Until now, she'd been awful at predicting other people's behavior, but the more she got to know Darthrok, the more qualified she felt to make predictive assessments. The same was true for Essley, and Sally wondered if she would get better at predicting Sujan, as well.

"Because Sujan is different. Maybe someone else is different, too."

He nodded, slowly at first, but faster as he thought about it. "Fair enough. You think maybe someone else could be like you?"

"Maybe. Maybe not. Or maybe someone else is like him. I want to see. Then maybe I can figure out what happened to me. Or why it happened."

"All right. Let's go. Essley's, uh, sleeping, I guess. She can catch up with us later."

Sally double-checked her store's notification system. *Yep. Working great.* She could see that she and Darthrok were in there. When they stepped out of the shop, the notifications updated to show an empty room.

So cool!

"Should we be systematic about it?" he suggested. "Just start at one spot and work our way all the way around town? It's probably the best way to meet the CMs who are always at their post."

Like she used to be. But not anymore! "Sure."

"We can just skip the ones you've already met."

She hoped they'd run into Tilly Hightower, but the odds didn't seem to be in her favor on that one. Tilly was probably out having a wild adventure with her band of toughs and thugs.

"Let's start at the jail," he suggested.

Sally stopped walking. "Why?"

"It's just a good starting point, the way the town is arranged right now. Is there something wrong with the jail?"

"Seems weird." Wouldn't it be suspicious for them to just show up to say howdy at a place for incarcerating criminals?

"Nah, it's fine. People go in to check the wanted notices. You can make some good money turning in people who've been caught breaking the law. You don't even have to be a mercenary to do bounty hunting. Anyone can do it and get the reward." He gestured for her to come with him and started walking.

"Okay." If people regularly walked into the jail to look at notices, then they shouldn't stick out. She really didn't want to attract any particular notice from anyone. If Somewhat Threatening Guy heard about it, he'd show up again.

She hadn't told Essley and Darthrok about him. She hadn't been able to find the right words at the time, and now that it had been a while since she'd seen the guy, she kind of just wanted to think that she didn't need to worry about him. She had plenty of other things to focus on, and she didn't think Somewhat Threatening Guy was a puzzle she could solve.

Not yet, anyway. She needed to learn a whole lot more before she could tackle that quest.

The jail looked a lot like the bank to Sally. Big and heavy, with a lot more wheels than Sally's store had. Less attractive than any of the shops, and somehow more formal.

Sally felt a twinge of nervousness about approaching a place filled with criminals, but Darthrok showed no concern at all, so she followed his lead, trying to play it cool.

A short entryway led into the jail's reception area. Somehow, she hadn't imagined that a jail had such a thing. She'd imagined...oh, she didn't really know. Crusty jailers who barked out orders and groups of people freestyle brawling. Or something.

In reality, the jail was quiet, orderly, and kind of peaceful. The floors were smooth and shiny, the walls looked expensive, and the man sitting at reception looked both intimidating and friendly.

An amazing combination. She wanted to learn how to do that.

Darthrok gave the Southern guy a nod and began studying the wanted notifications.

She'd expected actual posters, but these were digital screens that displayed a person's face, both straight-on and in profile, and their vital statistics. For a few minutes she stood motionless, watching the images change. As she was about to talk to the Southern reception guy, a familiar face flashed on the screen.

Kitria.

Sally's stomach rolled over and a shudder shook her whole body. What was this feeling? It was strong, and terrible. It wasn't anger. It wasn't fear. It was...revulsion.

Yes. She felt truly revolted by Kitria. She despised the woman who had abused her all those years. And she did recognize the behavior as abuse now. Before, she'd ignored it as an unpleasant, inevitable event. She'd been observing how adventurers treated other adventurers, though, and realized that the way Kitria behaved wasn't at all normal. Even though most adventurers ignored CMs or gave them the most cursory of attention, no one had ever been violent like Kitria.

Sally noted all the details of Kitria's criminal notice, and committed them to memory.

When she approached the reception guy, he looked up with a polished smile and said, "Hello. How can I help you?"

Sally liked all the regional ethnicities, but she admired Southerners' high intelligence and perception, and their aptitude for all professions. "Just wanted to say hello. It's my first time here. I'm Sally."

His smile widened. "Always nice to meet someone who has an interest in keeping our town free of crime. I'm Jayce Briggs. If you ever need help, let me know."

"That's kind of you, thanks."

"Don't mention it."

She smiled. "Okay, I won't."

He returned his attention to whatever he'd been looking at before she'd arrived. Sally rejoined Darthrok, who continued to watch the wanted notices.

"What did you think of the sheriff?" he asked without looking up.

Sally looked around. "Where?"

"You were talking to him."

"Really?" She looked back at Jayce, who bit the pad of his thumb as he scrutinized a paper.

"Yep. He keeps his appearance plain, he says, to fool hooligans into thinking he's nobody."

Sally nodded thoughtfully. "That makes sense."

"Did you feel anything different about him?"

She shrugged. "Not really. He's nice enough. That's all."

"Okay. Flower shop next?"

"Sure."

SALLY TOOK a huge bite of churro and chewed. The heavenly flavor that accompanied the sweetness, she'd learned, was called *cinnamon*. The doughy deliciousness took the edge off her disappointment.

"There are other towns," Darthrok said encouragingly. "Maybe the princess you're looking for is in another castle."

Sally stared at him as she chewed. With her mouth still full, she said, "Those aren't real things."

He smiled. "Not here, they aren't. It was just a joke."

She didn't pretend to laugh. Sometimes his jokes just weren't funny. Not to her, anyway.

"Anyway," Darthrok continued, looking amused, "What next? I thought Essley would be here by now, but she must have had something to do."

Sally took another bite of churro. They'd gone through all of Pivot, seeking out CMs. Four times, she'd doubled back to her store to help customers. After she'd made sure people had what they needed from her store, they'd picked up the tour where they'd left off.

She hadn't managed to touch a single one of the CMs, nor had any of them felt like they were similar to her. Each of them had been fairly simple, with obviously pre-established lines of dialogue.

That made her think of Sujan. He used plenty of set dialogue, but sometimes she felt like he was customizing things he said. Plus, she'd been able to touch him. *And*, she found it easier to talk to him. What made him different than the other CMs?

She stuffed the last of her churro in her mouth. "I need to talk to Sujan again."

Darthrok gazed at her, mystified. "What? I can't hear you with all that food in your mouth."

At first, putting the remainder of her food into her mouth had seemed efficient, because she wouldn't have to continue to hold it. Now that she'd done it, she found that having too much food in her mouth could make it, paradoxically, hard to chew or swallow.

With an effort, she managed to gulp the dessert down, noting that she'd need to keep her bites much smaller in the future. "Ow."

Darthrok laughed. "Let's get some water. It'll help wash

that down. Sometimes I forget how new you are to everything."

They backtracked to the tavern, which they'd already checked out. At the counter, Darthrok ordered two waters and slid two coppers across the bar.

Sally smiled politely at Lorrain, for whom, presumably the tavern had been named. "Last Call Lorrain's" was a fun name, really.

Lorrain nodded back at Sally pleasantly, but without any hint of recognition, even though Sally had talked to her at length just a half hour ago. The bartender didn't appear to find it odd that Sally and Darthrok would come in for drinks, leave, and come back again for water so soon.

"Can I get a lemonade?" Sally asked.

Lorrain brightened, with exactly the same toothy smile she'd shown when Darthrok had first ordered lemonades for them.

"One Lulu of a Lemonade coming up!"

While the bartender got the beverage, Darthrok asked, "Testing her out to see if you can get a different response?"

Sally sighed. She hadn't expected it to work. "Not really. Mostly, I just like the drink."

"We could get a spiked one, if you want to try it."

She shook her head. "I prefer it unpierced."

He laughed. "No, spiked means it has alcohol in it. You've never tried it, right?"

"I've heard of it. No thanks."

He finished off his water and set the glass down. "Fair enough. To be honest, the lemonade's tastier when it's plain."

Sally finished her water, and Lorrain set a tall, frosty glass with a slice of lemon on the rim in front of Sally.

Darthrok leaned his chin on his hand and watched her

take a drink. "It's funny about you. In some ways you're super smart and savvy, and in others, you're like a child. It's cute."

"I feel the same about you," she said, "but probably less cute."

He laughed, and she smiled in response. She liked that she could make jokes and tease him, and that he'd laugh. He had a good sense of humor. He was honest, and he'd proven to be trustworthy. He'd been a bit blunt and unintentionally insulting at first, but he treated her pretty much like he treated Essley now.

"What do you think about me?" she asked carefully, watching him. "Do you think I'm real?"

He blinked in surprise, then his expression turned thoughtful. "I'm not sure what you are, really. If you're sentient or what. I do think you're unique, and that whatever has made you the way you are now, it wasn't intentional. There's no way what you've been doing is part of anyone's plan. So...I believe you're Sally Strong. One of a kind." He ducked his head and smiled at her. "Is that good enough?"

She got a thrill out of hearing her new name, but her sense of warmth toward him went deeper than that. He didn't entirely understand her—and that was okay, because she didn't understand herself yet, either—but he was a friend she could count on, nonetheless.

"Good enough," she agreed.

She took a sip of her sweet, tangy lemonade, and her notification system alerted her that someone had just stepped into her shop.

"Is something wrong?" Darthrok asked.

"I have to go to my shop." She pushed her drink away, suddenly no longer interested in it.

"You could bring the lemonade with you," he suggested. "No need to get sad about it."

"It's not that. I just don't want to go."

"Why?"

She'd known this problem would come up sooner or later. She'd been hoping it would wait a bit longer. Until she felt more ready for it. "It's Kitria."

———

SALLY HAD NEVER FELT MORE worried about entering her shop. Normally, she knew exactly what would happen, and felt confident that she could handle any transaction with ease. A person would ask for something, Sally would provide it, and the world would continue to spin.

This was nothing like those times. As Sally entered her shop, she didn't know how the impending transaction would end. Or begin. Or what might happen in between.

She did know that it would be unlike anything else she'd experienced.

Breathing in the familiar scent of her store—all wood and metal and oil—she straightened her shoulders and walked behind the counter. Only then did she fasten her attention on Kitria.

Should she fasten on her normal, amiable smile? Should she act the way Kitria expected her to?

No.

It might be safer to do so. Sally didn't want people to realize she'd changed. She didn't want to attract attention. But she couldn't pretend to be what she used to be in front of Kitria. Sally was awake now, as awake as Kitria or Darthrok or anyone else, and she deserved better.

She deserved to defend herself.

Sally met Kitria's gaze, unsmiling. She put her hands on the sales counter that was in *her* store, which was situated in *her* town.

She leaned forward. "What do you want?"

Kitria's head tilted back and to the side. "That's a new greeting. Upgrades?"

Dathrok stood just inside the entry, tense. In that instant, Sally knew that if things went badly, he would fight, and die, for her. She also knew that Kitria could pound him into the dirt. He was only level twelve.

Sally did a deep assessment of Kitria rather than the usual basic type that only required a glance. She carefully noted every detail.

Kitria

Adventurer

Chaotic Neutral

Level Forty

Profession: Entrepreneur

Specialty: Mercenary

Kitria is carrying fifty-eight platinum coins.

Kitria has seventy-eight platinum, sixty-three gold, twenty-eight silver, and twelve copper in electronic funds.

Kitria is a formidable adversary, but not a concern for you.

Kitria is in a bad mood. Kitria is usually in a bad mood.

Sally laughed at that last bit. She leaned forward, toward Kitria, gathering all of her words and letters, and carefully enunciated. "Up grades. Big. Big up grades, Kitria, chaotic neutral level forty mercenary adventurer."

Wow, that was a lot of syllables. But she'd gotten through it.

Kitria's arrogance faded, and curiosity rushed in to replaced it. "Is an event about to start?"

Sally dug deep and gave Kitria her best look of disdain. "Are you going to tell me what you want?"

Kitria blinked. "Wow. I guess they changed your personality. Okay. Buy premium metal cutter."

Sally narrowed her eyes. "Ask nicely."

Kitria took a step back. "Dude, don't get a short circuit. What did they do to you? Fine. *Please* can I buy a premium metal cutter?"

Sally smiled. "Two platinum."

It was a fair price. Not the most she might charge, but not nearly as low as she could potentially offer, if an adventurer's karma and charisma were working in their favor.

"Offer one plat," Kitria said.

"People don't talk like that," Sally sniffed. "Ask nicely."

Kitria ran a hand through her hair. "Seriously? Fine, whatever. *Please*, can I *offer* one platinum for the *premium* metal cutter?"

Sally didn't like her tone, or the way she sarcastically enunciated every few words. "No. Two platinum."

Kitria scratched her chin and shifted her weight. "Are you wearing new clothes?"

Sally stared at her. Was Kitria only now paying attention to Sally, now that she'd stood up for herself?

She should have stood up for herself a long time ago. She wished she'd been able to do it a lot sooner, but it still felt good.

Kitria sighed. "Fine. Accept."

It wasn't a polite acceptance, as Kitria might have said to another adventurer, but Sally had pushed Kitria far enough for today. Sometimes, repairs took a long time to complete.

Sally reached beneath her counter and pulled out two identical cutters. One of them, she exchanged with Kitria for exactly two platinum coins.

The other, she activated and held in front of her, in case Kitria should get any ideas about reaching for her short sword.

Kitria's chin came up, her eyes focused on the dangerous tool.

Sally deactivated the tool and met Kitria's gaze. Really looked into her eyes. She leaned forward and enunciated, "*Happy adventuring. Come again soon.*"

For the first time ever, Sally saw a flicker of doubt in Kitria's eyes.

"This is weird." Kitria frowned. "Whatever."

She left the store.

As soon as she was out, Darthrok could no longer maintain his cool. He let out a wordless shout, then said, "Holy" and then a bizarre ululating sound came out of his mouth.

Sally stared at him.

"Sorry," he said. "Profanity filter. I mean, holy gasket, that was steamin' awesome! I'm pretty sure you made her fear for her life, and you didn't even do anything."

Sally laughed. "I did, didn't I?"

"Yeah, you did!" He ran around the counter and picked her up, spinning her around.

She laughed, he laughed, they both laughed until they were giddy with the thrill of success.

She heard the sound of a throat clearing, and Darthrok set her down.

"What did I miss?" Essley asked.

"AND SHE JUST LEFT?" Essley asked in disbelief.

"Walked right out," Darthrok confirmed, grinning.

"Wow. I wish I'd seen that." Essley's look of amazement gradually morphed into a smile.

Sally had let Darthrok do most of the storytelling, both because she didn't want to stumble over her words and because she wanted to hear his perspective.

His perspective made her sound *really* cool. So cool that she almost wanted to meet the person he was describing, but that person was her and she could scarcely believe it.

She giggled, suffused with a level of delight previously unknown to her.

Pride.

It was pride she felt. She'd known the word, but not the feeling. Until now.

An odd but pleasant sensation filled her, like light filling a previously darkened room. She felt brightened. Illuminated. Parts of her that had been dark now felt newly alive. She felt smarter, more aware, and more capable.

The sensation was similar to when she increased her knowledge. It had to mean that she'd leveled up.

She closed her eyes and pressed a hand to her chest, sinking into her sense of pride and accomplishment.

"Sally. Sally?" Essley's voice penetrated Sally's haze and she opened her eyes.

"You're crying again," Essley said, stepping close and wiping tears from her cheek.

Sally hadn't realized. "It's good," she assured her friends. "It isn't bad to cry. It's strong."

Darthrok leaned in and patted her on the back. "Yeah, it can be. Just like you."

She smiled. She'd never felt stronger. She wiped away the rest of her tears and slapped her hands down on her sales counter. "Right. Sally Strong, phase two."

She struggled to say the word *phase*, which she'd put

together with sounds from different words, but from Essley's and Darthrok's expressions, they understood it.

"Sure," Darthrok agreed. "So what's phase two?"

"All circuits that lead in also lead out," Sally said.

"Okay. Same question." He smiled faintly.

Sally smiled back. "We wake Sujan."

8

      ———

"How do you know Sujan can be woken?" Essley held her hands up in front of her in an apologetic gesture, palms out. "Don't take that the wrong way. But he doesn't seem like he's...you know...like you."

It was true, Sally's plan had a major flaw, but she wasn't going to let that slow her down. The worst that could come of her trying to wake Sujan was that he would remain unawake.

A little bit of failure wouldn't hurt her.

"He isn't like me," Sally admitted. "Yet. But if I can, I think he can. I'm different than everyone. But he's different too, in his own way. I can touch him."

"That *is* different," Darthrok agreed. "But he isn't awake like you. He's still moving in his old patterns. Following his same loops."

"But I can *touch* him," Sally persisted. "I can't touch the other CMs. And my words are bigger with him. To talk is easy."

"Plus, he's gorgeous, right, Sal?" Essley grinned. "I mean, he's not my type, but he's very good looking."

Sally smirked and shook her head. "That doesn't hurt, but it's not why."

Essley and Darthrok chuckled.

"So how do we wake him?" Darthrok asked.

"Don't know." Sally pursed her lips. "That's the weak spot."

"That's the weak spot in the plan?" Essley peered at her for confirmation.

Sally nodded.

"Yeah, I'd say so." Darthrok frowned thoughtfully.

"There was a guy," Sally said slowly.

They both looked at her expectantly, waiting for more.

"A kind of scary guy," she added.

Essley nodded encouragingly.

Sally focused on her words and letters, carefully planning each word and syllable before she said them. It was hard, and her sentences became very slow. "GM, may be. He talked to me. He knew I was different. He said he could give me more words, but said I needed to be fixed. So I acted like old Sally Streetmonger to make him go away."

Darthrok threw his hands up in the air. "Hang on, hang on, wait. A GM noticed that you'd changed and talked to you about it?"

Sally nodded.

"And he said he could increase your vocabulary, but that he wanted to make you the way you used to be?"

Sally nodded again.

"Blazing currents, Sally, how did you not mention this before?" Darthrok's eyes were much wider than normal.

"He went away," she answered. "Is it important still?"

Darthrok's eyes got even bigger. "Yeah! Yeah, that'd be important. Even if he thought you'd been reset, he's likely to check back on you to make sure your code's clean."

He was saying strange words again, and he seemed upset.

"What should we do?" she asked.

"There's nothing to do, really," Essley said. "If we try asking about it, we'll just be drawing attention to you, which we don't want."

"So," Sally said, "we can't do anything anyway. It doesn't factor in."

Essley and Darthrok exchanged a look.

"She's right," Essley said. "It doesn't change anything we might do."

"But it's something we should have known," Darthrok argued. "Sally, if something—if anything—happens, anything out of the ordinary, make sure you tell us, okay? Maybe it won't change anything about what we do, but at least we'll be informed, so we can be watching or thinking ahead. Even if the words are hard for you to find, just try, and we'll try to understand. Okay?"

Aw. He was worried about her. She could tell. She nodded. "Okay."

It was nice to have someone worry about her.

She said, "I'm going to go see Sujan tomorrow."

"What will you do?" Essley asked. "Do you have any ideas on how to wake him up?"

Sally shook her head. "No ideas yet. Maybe I'll think of something. Or maybe Guy will show up."

Essley looked concerned about that possibility. "That could be a bad thing, though, right?"

"Could be," Sally admitted. "If it happens, we'll see. Otherwise, I'll keep working on Sujan."

She had about twelve hours. She needed to come up with a new, very convincing reason for him to take her on as an apprentice. If she fulfilled the quest he'd given her, she'd have a reason to see him frequently. Spending time with him would give her the chance to find the key to waking him up. Plus, becoming his apprentice might make him more open to her. More accessible.

Sally looked from Essley to Darthrok. "He's different than the others, and Guy wants us to stay apart. That has to mean something, right?"

"It could." Essley nodded.

"Sure, why not?" Darthrok agreed.

They weren't entirely convinced. She could see from their body language that they were keeping their doubts to themselves to avoid discouraging her.

Should she reconsider? She didn't want Somewhat Threatening Guy around, and she definitely didn't want him tinkering with anything that made her who she now was. But everything seemed to be pointing her at Sujan, and she felt certain that there must be a reason.

Adventuring was *supposed* to be risky, right?

SALLY'S FINGERS felt jittery as she rang the bell to Sujan's shop. She'd manufactured a reason to make an appointment with him, and hoped it would be enough.

Enough to become his apprentice, at the very least.

The door unlocked and she took a deep breath before opening it.

"Oh, it's you." His bored, somewhat disapproving observation made her nervousness evaporate and reignited her cheekiness. Why did he make her want to annoy him?

"Yes," she agreed in an overly sweet tone, "which makes sense, considering I'm the one who made the appointment."

If he noticed her sarcasm, he didn't show it. "Since you

made an appointment, I assume you came here for more than sightseeing. Care to get to the point?"

He'd made that exact same remark about sightseeing last time. He was definitely going through one of his behavior loops.

"Be my mentor." She hoped that somehow, he'd now find her worthy of his teaching.

He arched an eyebrow. "You have to prove yourself worthy of my teaching."

She sighed. He'd said that before, too. She hadn't expected him to make this easy. But then, she wasn't planning to make it easy for him, either. "I'm staying here until you accept me."

The eyebrow arched higher, making him look terribly arrogant. She wanted to force that look off his face.

"I don't teach just anyone," he said.

"Well, good," she retorted. What was it about him that activated all her contrariness? "Because I'm not just anyone. I'm Sally Strong. I'm different than anyone else."

"Is that right?" He crossed his arms over his chest.

"Yes! It is! Have you seriously not noticed anything different about me? You're so smart, according to you. A master technie, right? So take a deeper look at me. Do I seem like other adventurers? Do you really not see how different I am?"

He assessed her. "Sally Strong. Mid-level technie. You look like you'd give me a good fight. You are not yet apprenticed to anyone."

He gave her a pointed, yet somehow bored look to prove how unimpressed he was.

"Let's start with that." She crossed her arms over her chest, mimicking his posture, and took a step back, half-sitting on an empty worktable.

"That's not a chair," he said tersely.

"Nope, it sure isn't." Since it seemed to bother him, she scooted her behind further back and let her feet dangle off the floor. "But I don't have to do what you say, since you aren't my mentor."

She smiled sweetly, then continued. "You said I'm Sally Strong. But that wasn't my name when I last met you. Remember? You identified me as only Sally. I had only one name then, like an adventurer, but now I have two. How do you explain that?"

"Your personal affairs are not my concern." His tone was cold, but the slight furrow in his brow showed uncertainty.

"You can't explain it, right? Because it doesn't fit Everternian mechanics. Doesn't that bother you, Mr. Master Technie?"

He frowned at her, clearly displeased.

"And how about the part about me being a 'mid-level technie?'" she pressed. "That's awfully vague. When I assess people, I see their actual level. Don't you usually see people's exact levels?"

"Understanding my customer helps me understand my customer's needs," he answered.

"I'll take that as a yes," she said, pleased. "So why is it you think you can't see my levels? Who else in this world can you *not* see levels for? What type of people?"

She waited for him to think about it. When CMs looked at other CMs, they didn't see number ranks. Not for levels or skills or anything else. Because CMs didn't have things like that. As a CM, neither did Sally. Not the kind that she or Sujan could see, anyway. But she did gain experience, which CMs weren't supposed to do.

Could he see that in her, and if he did, could he reason out why that might be?

"Look at me," she urged. "Really look at me. Think about what pieces fit, and which ones don't."

He hesitated and she enjoyed his indecision. He was struggling to find a reasonable explanation and failing.

"And what about that notification device you helped me with?" she continued. "It was for my store, right? If I'm an adventurer, how do I have a store? That's not possible. Adventurers have to partner with a CM entrepreneur in order to put their goods in a store. It encourages competition among adventurers to be better, and keeps poor-quality goods out of the shops, right?" She raised her voice. "So how do I have a store, Sujan?"

He frowned, and she could see him trying to figure it out.

"Come on," she cajoled. "It's like a puzzle. Like a machine. Every piece is supposed to fit together, to work properly, right? So what does it mean if I have some parts of me that are CM, and some that are adventurer?"

She held her breath, hoping he'd put the facts together and figure it out.

His lips pressed into a thin line. "I have work to do."

He crossed the room and opened a storage bin.

Sally jumped off the table and went to stand beside him. "And what about this?"

With her fingertip, she gently touched the flat, dark mole behind his ear. As before, she felt no connection. He didn't become part of her group, nor could she initiate a private conversation bubble with him. But she could feel the warmth of his skin.

"Is there anyone else who can touch you?" she asked.

He stared at her, his expression unreadable.

She reached for his hand, hoping that she'd be able to grab it this time.

He pulled away. "I have work to do."

Sally's shoulders slumped. She straightened them. "Fine. You work. I'll watch. And we'll do this all over again when you're done."

He didn't glance at her as he began taking tools from one of the storage bins.

WAS SHE MAKING A MISTAKE?

Almost a day later, Sally was still haunting Sujan. He'd taken to ignoring her unless she got directly in his way. Her store had logged twelve customers ringing the doorbell, then going away when it wasn't answered.

She felt really bad that her plan was impacting her store. She didn't want to keep him from doing his job, either.

Maybe she'd made a bad decision.

But if she left, Sujan would have no reason to accept her as his apprentice, and if he didn't do that, she had no reason to interact with him on a daily basis. And without seeing him, how was she supposed to get him to wake up?

The more time she spent with him, the more strongly she felt that she could wake him. That she *needed* to wake him.

He wasn't like Ginny from Bracket or Mr. Barrowman from the bank or Sheriff Jayce. He wasn't like any of the other CMs. He was more adaptable. The way he talked was more sophisticated. Not his tone or his actual words, but his engagement in the conversation and ability to understand things outside of his normal loops. There was something familiar about the way he behaved.

Plus, she could touch him. That had to mean something. Didn't it?

Plus, he liked the puzzle of putting machines together and taking them apart to fix them. The fact that he and Sally both liked that kind of thing couldn't be a coincidence. Could it?

Restlessly, she paced across the workshop. She'd already memorized the placement of the tools hanging on the wall and the storage bins' content labels.

Unfortunately, Sujan's tidiness meant that there was nothing out for her to poke about with, and she felt like taking anything out of its place without permission would be unforgivably rude.

She liked antagonizing Sujan, but she wasn't a jerk. She observed him whenever he was working, but he seemed to have a habit of staring at his work for long intervals without actually doing anything, except for maybe thinking really hard.

She doubted he was engaged in deep thought, though. She suspected that sitting at a worktable with something in front of him was his default activity when he was unneeded for anything else. Just as she had wiped her shop counter to pass the time, in the days before she'd woken up and started having her own thoughts and desires about things.

He was just sitting there. Staring at a communicator device. Probably not thinking a single thing.

It was creepy. She didn't like it.

"Hey, Sujan!" she called impulsively.

He blinked and turned his head slowly to look at her, his eyes dull and unfocused.

Wow. Super creepy.

Then his eyes seemed to brighten and actually see her, making him seem normal again. "Yes?"

She hadn't thought further than calling his name, and

she'd barely even thought about that part. Sometimes her impulsiveness got her into sticky situations.

She went with the first thing that came to mind. "What do you call a fake noodle?"

He frowned slightly, then shrugged. "I don't know. What do you call a fake noodle?"

Sally beamed at him. "An impasta!"

He eyed her warily. "Okay."

"It's a joke. A riddle. Riddles are like teeny little puzzles. Want to try another?"

"No."

But she wanted to make him think outside his normal parameters, and try to get him to say things he wouldn't normally say. "What do you call a crushed right angle?"

He put his hand to his chin. "Geometry?"

"Kind of. But not really." She smiled sweetly.

"Is this a design problem you're having?"

She grinned. "No. It's another riddle."

He squinted at her, then shrugged. "What's the answer?"

"A wrecked angle. Get it? Rectangle?"

"You're a very strange person," he said.

His lips twitched.

"Hah! You do get it!" she crowed. Encouraged, she said, "How warm is a janitor's closet?"

He quirked his shoulders questioningly.

"Broom temperature."

He grimaced. "That's just bad."

Sally giggled. "Yeah, you're right. Okay. How many passive-aggressive people does it take to screw in a lightbulb?"

Looking pained, he asked, "How many?"

"Just one," she retorted. "But that's fine. I'm sure the other person had *much* more important things to do."

His lips twitched again.

"Your turn," she said. "You tell me one."

"I don't know any."

"You're a maker, right? A master technie? Surely you can make a tiny little riddle. Can't you?"

She widened her eyes, as if concerned. "I mean, if you can't even do that..." She let her voice trail off.

He looked down at his hands. Was he going back into standby mode?

Then he smoothed his shirt front and took a breath. "I went to the doctor for surgery. He said he could put me to sleep with gas or a big rock. I said either ore."

Sally waited him to finish the joke, but he didn't. Well, it was only his first try. Maybe with some practi—

She caught onto his wordplay.

"Either *ore*," she repeated, then burst into giggles. "That's terrible. But funny because it's terrible. Good job."

He smiled. For the first time, it was a real smile with no condescension or sarcasm.

It was a such a nice smile that she couldn't help but smile back. She willed him to wake up and be his own person. "Try. Please just try."

He gazed at her, a calculating look in his eyes. "Very well."

"What?" Sally blinked at him.

"I'll give you a trial as my apprentice. But if you fail, you have to give up the idea. I don't take on just anyone."

Sally let out a slow breath. It was a success, although not exactly what she'd been hoping for.

But it was a step in the right direction.

"Okay," she agreed. "When do we start?"

"Tomorrow. Noon. Be prepared."

"Oh, I'll be prepared," she promised. "You be prepared."

She flashed him a challenging expression.

He smiled. "See you tomorrow, Sally Strong."

"Wow, two real smiles from you in one day," she mused. "What will tomorrow bring?"

Happily, she hurried back to her store to deal with the customers who were waiting for her.

"WHAT ABOUT THAT guy you told us about?" Darthrok asked. "The GM or whatever. Don't you think spending so much time with Sujan, and spending so much time out of your store, might get his attention?"

"It could," Sally admitted. She slowly put away the bundle of scrap parts she'd just purchased from an adventurer. She dawdled over the task to buy herself little more time to decide how she was going to answer Darthrok. "But I have to live, don't I? If I don't, then what's the point of being awake?"

He cracked his knuckles nervously. "Yeah, I get it. And I don't blame you. I'm just...worried. I don't want anything to happen to you. It's only been a few weeks, but you've become my favorite reason for being here."

Sally leaned forward and patted his shoulder. "You're one of my favorites, too."

He laughed. "Right. Thanks. Anyway, Essley should be here anytime. She said she had a surprise."

"I love surprises." Sally always liked seeing Essley, but with a surprise promised, she looked forward to it even more.

"I know. So." He ran a hand along the edge of the counter. "What do we do while we wait?"

She didn't think he'd be interested in studying her books

with her, which was what she normally did between customers. She looked at him slyly. "Do you, perhaps, have any puzzles to sell?"

"Of course not. I'd have mentioned that first. But are you suggesting I buy one?"

Sally smiled. He was getting smarter.

Taking her smile as his answer, he asked, "Okay. I'd like to buy a puzzle. What's your best one?"

Sally shot him a look of approval before whirling to her cabinets and pulling out a large puzzle made of a variety of different colored metals. Carefully, she set it on the counter.

"Wow. I've never seen one this big. It's almost as big as your cash register. Where did you get this?"

"A high-level enforcer mercenary." She added, "Don't really know him. But this is a special quest item."

"Nice. How much?"

She felt around in her senses to determine the lowest price she could offer him. As a very rare item, she couldn't give it away for a nominal coin or two. She had to legitimately sell it to him for at least a platinum for the transaction mechanics to work. This puzzle was something special, though, she was certain. If anyone but Essley or Darthrok wanted to purchase it, she wouldn't accept less than twenty plat.

"For you, one plat." She gave him a sly grin. "Don't tell your friends."

He smiled at her choice of familiar wording. "It's a good deal, I'm sure. But even though I've been working hard to earn money, that would just about wipe me out. And I've been saving up for some armor..."

He trailed off, then shook his head. "Never mind. The armor will be there later. If you think I should do this puzzle, then let's do it!"

Sally locked her gaze on him and did a deep assessment. She'd always been capable of studying an adventurer hard enough to know how much money they had in the bank, but since waking up she rarely did. Not only did money not concern her, but she also didn't want to be intrusive.

She wanted to look out for her friend, though. If his funds ran too low, he wouldn't be able to afford healing or necessary supplies.

Focusing carefully on him, she saw that his bank account had the plat but that was almost all. He'd be left with pocket change.

"I'll run to the bank. Be right back," he said. He could transfer the funds to her electronically, of course, but she'd have to take an additional surcharge. With the bank so nearby, there was no reason for him not to get the coin in hand to save himself the extra cost.

She put a hand on his arm and gestured at his neck. "Wait. What's that?"

"What?" His eyes widened, touching his jaw, then the side of his face.

She reached out toward his ear then pulled her arm back, revealing a platinum coin. "You have the money right here."

She dropped the coin in his palm, and he stared at it dumbly for a long moment.

"You do sleight of hand coin tricks now?" he asked.

Sally shrugged modestly. "Training my fine motor skills. For when I work on machines with tiny parts."

She'd begun practicing with her hands after seeing Sujan working on that pocket watch. She'd realized then she didn't have the dexterity to begin something so complex. So far, concealing the coin under her thumb was all she could do, but she'd keep working on it.

His hand closed around the coin. "Thanks, Sally."

If he suspected that money was nothing to her, he didn't let on.

He held the coin out to her. "One puzzle, please!"

They grinned at each other, then she accepted the coin and gestured to the puzzle. "All yours."

He studied the thing, leaning first one way then the other for a different view of it. "Okay, so it's got all these rectangular pieces, and each one is painted one color on one side, and a different color on the other." He muttered to himself as he poked a green-and-blue colored piece, turning it carefully on a horizontal axis. "And the colors aren't all the same, or all different."

The metal piece gave a tiny click with the blue side up.

"And they seem to move into place." He turned the piece again, clicking it into place with the green side up. "Hmm."

He glanced up at her. "Do you already know the answer?"

"No. I've never seen one like this."

"That makes me feel a little better." He returned his attention to the puzzle. "This might take a while."

Sally watched him with interest as he moved around the thing, turning the rectangular bits this way and that, looking for a pattern.

Essley arrived. "Hey, guys. What's that?"

She approached the counter curiously.

Sally didn't follow her friend's gaze, but looked intently at Essley. Something was different.

When she assessed Essley, she no longer saw Essley as a mercenary.

Essley
Adventurer
Neutral Good

Level Twelve/Level Two
Profession 1 (frozen): Entrepreneur
Profession 2 (active): Maker
Specialty: Botanist
Essley is carrying four copper coins.
Essley has two platinum, twenty-eight gold, zero silver, and seven copper in electronic funds.
Essley poses no threat to you.
Essley's karma is very good.
Essley looks like the kind of person who helps old ladies cross the street.

Sally laughed at the last bit. She needed to do more deep assessments to see more of those odd little lines.

"You retrained!" she exclaimed.

Previously absorbed in studying the puzzle, Darthrok turned his attention to Essley. "Whoa. Big change."

Essley nodded, looking shy but excited. "I thought about it a lot and decided that Sally was right."

Darthrok looked from her to Sally and back, raising an eyebrow in question.

Essley added, "She said that I could take the easier route and never be happy, or commit to the retrain, do the hard work, and be happy."

"I did?" Sally recalled the conversation, but didn't remember saying that.

"Well," Essley said, "maybe not in those words exactly, but that was the gist. It's no fun finding mechanical beasts to beat on, over and over. I want to make things instead. I have a lot of work to get my crafting skills up equal to my mercenary skills, so I can learn crafting at a normal rate. The half-rate learning penalty's going to be a real killer."

"We'll help," Sally said. "You'll get there."

Darthrok nodded in agreement. "So, what can you make?"

Essley grimaced, then laughed. "So far, just a really bad vitamin drink. It tastes awful, smells worse, and does almost nothing to increase energy. Basically, it's one grade above bog slime. But it's a way to practice."

"Sounds good," Darthrok said. When Essley gave him a weird look, he added quickly, "I mean, not the potion. That sounds awful, and I'm not going to volunteer to drink it until you're better at it. But the practicing is good. It'll be cool to have a botanist to adventure with."

"You aren't mad that we won't be able to hunt together like we did?" Essley asked hesitantly.

"Nah, what am I, some kind of jerk?" He mock-scowled at her. "Once we get your skills up, it'll be great. One merc, one botanist, one technie. That's a heckin' good adventuring party right there."

Essley smiled. "Yeah, it is. I should have started out that way."

"Live and learn," Darthrok said. "And you'll keep your combat ranks, so you'll be much better at fighting than most makers. Pretty cool."

Essley looked relieved. "Yeah, that'll be fun."

She gestured to the puzzle. "So what's this?"

"Sally sold me a quest puzzle. I don't even know where to start with it." Rather than show frustration, he smiled good-naturedly.

"You could pay her to help solve it," Essley suggested.

Darthrok peered closer at the puzzle and pushed it experimentally with his forefinger. "I might. But I want to try working at it first. It's rare, and would be pretty cool if I could figure it out myself. Is that okay, Sally? I bet you're eager to figure it out, and could do it way faster than me."

Sally shook her head. "Mystery is good. You keep trying."

Now that her friends were both there, she was more interested in sharing her news with them than fussing over the puzzle, however intriguing it was. She leaned forward and said, "Guess what?"

"What?" Darthrok and Essley asked, almost in unison.

"Sujan said yes," she announced triumphantly.

Darthrok said, "Yes to...wait, yes to being your mentor?"

Sally nodded excitedly. "A try out, to show him I can do it."

"Wow!" Essley hopped up and down. "He rarely accepts anyone. Mostly, people just find a mentor from another town. What did you do to impress him?"

Sally scrunched her nose, wondering what had finally done it. Her persistence, her ability to improvise, or maybe how fast she was learning? Those might be factors, but she was pretty sure they weren't the deciding one. "I made him laugh."

Essley and Darthrok stared at her.

"You what?" Darthrok asked. "He laughed?"

Sally nodded.

"Wow," he said slowly, amazed. "I didn't think it was possible. You know what, Sally? If you can pull off a feat like making Sujan Souk laugh, you might just be able to accomplish *anything* in this world."

Sally laughed, knowing he was only joking. On the other hand...she was eager to see just how far she could push her boundaries.

And she had two amazing friends to help her do it.

9

SALLY FROWNED at the metal disk in front of her, and the sandpaper she'd rubbed nearly smooth. When she'd imagined an apprenticeship with Sujan, it hadn't been like this. While she didn't mind menial labor, no matter how repetitive, he hadn't offered to actually teach her anything.

And it had been four whole days! Four days of running over to his shop and doing whatever he told her, and racing back to her own store whenever a customer arrived.

She'd spent that fourth day in his workshop, sanding metal to clean off impurities prior to welding. *By hand.* Because...well, she had no idea why when there were plenty of belt sanders in the shop.

It felt pretty heckin' pointless.

Maybe on the fifth day he'd show her some welding. That would be exciting. All fiery and melty and weldy.

On the fifth day, she replaced the belts on the sanders. All day.

On the sixth day, she inventoried the drill bits, noting which ones would need to be replaced soon.

On the tenth day, she dusted. All day long.

"Dust is the worst enemy of technology," Sujan lectured. "Along with water."

So, she dusted.

On the fifteenth day, he pointed at a workbench near the window. "You can use that one when you have something to work on."

But he gave her nothing to work on.

When the twentieth day rolled around, Sally arrived at Sujan's workshop planning to make a stand. To demand some actual teaching. What was the point of a trial apprenticeship if he wasn't even going to teach her anything? What was he the mentor of? Tidying up?

"Hello, Sally." He looked up as she let herself in.

"You have to teach me something," she stated without even greeting him first. "Today."

Feeling like she needed to somehow emphasize her words, she crossed her arms over her chest.

Hmph.

He smiled faintly and tilted his chin up, in the direction of the window.

Sally looked and saw an array of parts arranged on her workbench alongside a variety of tools neatly laid out at right angles.

"Today, you'll build a basic motor," he said. "Since you've proven your dedication."

Was that what she'd done with all those boring tasks? "Well...okay!"

She sat down and they began their first lesson.

"Ugh." Essley leaned against the wall of Sally's store and slid down it until she was in a sitting position. She put her face in her hands. "Grinding out levels stinks."

Darthrok sat next to her and nudged her with an elbow. "At least you're on your way. Level five already."

The three of them had taken to meeting up at Sally's after their daily activities, since those were taking them all in different directions for the moment.

"I guess. But each level gets progressively harder, so it just gets slower and slower." She looked over to Sally. "How's the apprenticeship going? It's probably a lot like what I'm going through."

Sally stood behind her counter, feeling a little awkward with her friends sitting on the floor and over to the side. She crossed the room and sat down opposite them. She needed to get some chairs or something. This was not fancy. Or even comfortable.

"It's slow but not boring," Sally said. "I like learning. Don't you?"

"Well, yeah." Essley shifted. "But right now I'm just hunting plants, then grinding them to turn them into drinks, ointments, and poultices. Over and over and over. And over. It's repetitive."

"What exactly is a poultice?" Darthrok asked. "I always thought it was a fun word. Poultice. Poultice. Like poultry, but only sort of because there aren't any chickens."

Essley sent him a withering look. "It's a mashed-up goop of plants that you smear on skin and lay a cloth over. Usually while it's warm. That's all."

"Oh." He looked disappointed. "I thought it was something more...I don't know. Specific."

"The specifics depend on the purpose of the poultice. They can be very beneficial. Or at least mine will be once

I've gained enough skill. Right now, you'd mostly just be wearing some warm oatmeal on your leg."

He grimaced. "Pass."

Essley shifted her gaze to Sally. "I'm glad your work is more rewarding."

"No rewards yet," Sally answered. "But I'm learning. It's tough to run back here all the time, though."

Darthrok made a sympathetic hum. "I bet that stinks. Just when you get going on a project, bam, someone wants to buy some boots or something."

"Yeah." Sally wished she could post hours for her store or work only by appointment like Sujan did, but the store's mechanics made that impossible. It had to be open all the time, whether she was there or not.

"Too bad you can't hire someone." Darthrok smiled and joked, "Or take an apprentice of your own."

Sally smiled. An apprentice with an apprentice. That would be funny.

"Hang on." Darthrok looked down at the floor, in deep thought. "Yeah, why not?"

He pointed at Sally. "You're an entrepreneur/Maker CM who has a store." He pointed at Essley. "She's an adventurer maker who can partner with a storemonger. Why not?"

Sally stared at him. "I can't take an apprentice."

"Why not?" He pressed. "You have the skill, position, and the means."

She *had* partnered with some crafters, on occasion, selling their goods in her store for a commission of the price. But an apprentice was something else. No one had ever asked to learn how to clean counters and work the cash register.

Sally gazed at Essley, who looked as surprised by the idea as Sally felt.

"Could that work?" Essley asked. "I mean, if it could... that would be interesting. Wouldn't it?"

"Would you want to?" Sally asked tentatively.

"I think so. You'd be able to teach me at an accelerated rate, right? Even though you aren't a botanist, you could teach me some crafting skills, and the learning bonus would really help mitigate some of the drag caused by my dual-classing." Essley bit her lip as she thought. "And it would help you out, which is good. I mean, I could just as easily be here minding the store while I'm grinding away at making healing elixirs. If it could work, I mean. If I'd be able to sell your merchandise to people."

"It's a crazy idea," Sally said slowly, thinking about the systems Essley would have to be able to access and whether those permissions could be assigned to her.

"Crazy enough to work?" Darthrok asked hopefully.

"Maybe." Sally fixed all her attention on Essley. "Are you sure? Do you want to try?"

Essley nodded. "Yeah! Let's give it a try, at least. If it works, and I turn out to be a terrible employee, you can always just fire me."

Darthrok laughed, but Sally was too focused to spare any thought on humor. She thought hard about apprenticeship and becoming a mentor, which triggered a decision tree, opening up selectable options. She wasn't sure what all of them meant. Some didn't even appear to be written in any Everternian language. Some were just a jumble of numbers and dots.

Then she found an option that said: *Accept apprentice.*

She reached out and took Essley's hands. "Ask me to be your mentor."

"Um, okay. Sally, will you be my mentor, and, uh, let me be your apprentice?"

Darthrok let out a theatrical sigh and shook his head in disgust. "Fail. Man, you had a moment to say a really grand line, too. Maybe even do a big speech. You totally lamed out."

Essley glared at him, but ruined the effect with a slight smile.

An option lit up bright green in Sally's mind, and she selected it.

Accept Essley as my apprentice.

The decision tree bloomed with branches that had yet more branches leading out. Most of them, she couldn't decipher. Maybe that was because, like apprenticeship, it wasn't relevant at the time. Had she always had all of this inside her, just lying dormant and waiting for her to access it? How strange.

She wanted to study it all, to read and log all the branches, and puzzle out what the ones she couldn't understand were for. She wanted to understand it all.

A repetitive noise teased at the edge of her focus, and she tried to keep tuning it out, but the harder she tried, the louder and more insistent it became. Again, again, again, the same sound.

Reluctantly, she turned her attention toward it.

"Sally. Sally. Sally. What's going on?"

Essley looked scared. No, terrified.

Darthrok did, too.

"What?" Sally asked. "What happened?"

They both showed relief, but their worry didn't fade away.

"You went kind of...passive," Essley said. "You know, not quite here."

Sally looked from one to the other, trying to figure it out.

Then it hit her. "Did I seem like I did before I was awake? Like I wasn't all the way...here?"

"Yeah, something like that," Darthrok said. "You kind of froze up. What happened?"

Sally straightened. "I accepted Essley as apprentice. I started looking at options. Too many options. I think I got a little lost."

Darthrok licked his lips. "Okay, I'm not going to lie, that worries me. A lot."

"Did we break you?" Essley asked.

"Not broken." Sally gave herself a once-over, and she seemed fine. "I'll have to be careful."

"Should we not do the mentor thing?" Essley asked, anxious. "We probably shouldn't have tried that."

"No, it's fine," Sally insisted. "I just have to be careful not to look too far. I didn't know. Now I know. It's okay."

Their expressions eased somewhat.

"Okay," Darthrok said, "but if anything else like that happens, just try to get out of it fast and make sure you tell us about it. You'll do that, right?"

Sally nodded. "I'll do that. I'll be careful. I'm still learning."

She smiled to reassure them, then stood and dusted herself off. "Good. So, let's get started, apprentice!"

Essley smiled and her tension disappeared. "Right! Teach me, oh great mentor, for I am your student and together, there's nothing we can't accomplish." She sneaked a look at Darthrok. "How was that?"

"Stinky." He wore a pained expression. "So poor, so uninspired that I can almost actually smell it, like a physical stench." He dabbed at his eyes. "Ow. They burn."

Essley rolled her eyes, then hurried over to the cash register. "Think I can touch it now?"

She held up a finger, poised.

"I think you'd be a useless, bad employee if you couldn't," Darthrok answered.

Essley lowered the finger and put it on a cash register button. "Look at that!"

Sally smiled. She was glad Essley was pleased. She doubted her new apprentice would be so happy when Sally began teaching her the ins and outs of valuating scrap metal and other parts, and how to stay on top of supply and demand trends.

"YOU'RE GOOD, THOUGH?" Sally asked.

"I'm good. Everything's good. The store is in good hands. If anything comes up, I can just ping you since you have your shiny new communicator. Right?" Essley stood behind the counter of Sally's store, looking ready.

But was she? Retail could get crazy sometimes. Did Essley know that?

Sally hesitated.

"Go." Essley made a shooing gesture toward the door. "Sujan will be waiting for you. He's unpleasant when you're late, right?"

Sally grimaced. Essley's words were too true. The man had not warmed up one bit since she'd become his apprentice. If anything, he took his duties as her mentor even more seriously. She hadn't even been able to lure him into jokes and wordplay again. A shame, since he'd really lit up that one time.

He was really boring sometimes. But he had so much to teach her that she didn't truly mind. Learning wasn't supposed to be about constant excitement.

"I'll call you if anything unexpected comes up," Essley added in a soothing voice.

Still, Sally hesitated. She'd absorbed a whole lot of change lately, and delighted in it even. But somehow, handing her store operations off to someone else felt like a dereliction of duty. She knew Essley could handle the basic transactions that she had the authority to perform. As of yet, she couldn't valuate scrap to purchase, but she could sell any basic items that weren't puzzles. Puzzles remained entirely Sally's domain.

Sally fought a sense of guilt rather than any doubt in her friend's abilities. She felt a duty to her customers and feared that, in taking an apprentice to handle basic sales, she was failing as a storemonger.

This was "Sally's Store." Shouldn't she, Sally, be the one ensuring her customers' satisfaction? She'd always prided herself on that. Equipping adventurers, especially new adventurers, was the purpose of her existence.

Was she wrong to change things? To want more?

Essley came around the counter and took Sally's left hand in her right hand, with her other hand going to Sally's shoulder in a supportive touch. "I know it's hard, and probably scary, to do things that are so different. But everything's going to be okay. You're following your heart, and learning and growing. That's good. Don't second-guess it."

Relief swirled through Sally. Essley understood. This wasn't about whether Essley could do the job. It was about Sally letting go of something she felt solely responsible for so that she could forge ahead and see what she was capable of. "I'm not selfish?"

Essley smiled. "Of course not. Everyone deserves to reach for their dreams. You don't owe it to anyone to be what they want you to be. And if that Somewhat Threatening Guy comes around, I'll poke him in the eye for you."

She made an eye-poking gesture, which was so silly that Sally had to laugh.

Essley nodded toward the door. "Go. Be. Do. Live."

"Go, be, do, live," Sally repeated, feeling heartened. "Okay. I will."

With a rush of gratitude, she hugged her friend, her apprentice, and the person who right now was giving her the energy to push forward with something hard.

She pulled away and hurried out the door before she could second-guess these happy thoughts.

SALLY RETURNED to her store feeling uncharacteristically tired after a long day of Sujan testing her with break-fix problems. She smiled at Essley as she entered, stepping aside to let a customer exit. "How was today?"

"Good. Sold mostly basic goods, plus a couple of higher-quality items. I'm getting better at haggling. My ranks are improving so much, I'll probably level tomorrow." Essley looked quite pleased.

Over the past couple of weeks as Essley eased into handling the shop in Sally's absence, Sally had realized how hard the choice to retrain really had been for her friend. Essley struggled hard, with the goal of getting back to level twelve. Once she got there, she could overcome the learning penalties she'd taken on.

Essley hadn't said much about it at the time, but going from level twelve to level one had been tough for her. Sally was getting better at identifying and understanding unspoken feelings, and did her best to teach Essley as much as she could to try to mitigate the negatives Essley was experiencing.

That was friendship, wasn't it? Seeing a friend's penalties, and making an effort to help. Essley had been Sally's very first friend, and as much as Sally wanted to become a master technie, she was equally invested in being a master friend.

Maybe even more so.

"What's it like to level?" Sally asked, carefully forming the syllables into a proper sentence. She was getting a little better at that, during calm times. She liked being able to say normal sentences like other people did.

Essley's eyebrows rose in surprise. "Leveling? I guess that would be a mystery to you, huh? Sometimes I forget how different your experience here is compared to mine." She pursed her lips thoughtfully. "Well...leveling is great. A rush. First, it's the thrill of having accomplished something and getting the reward, then I get the advancements of increased levels or bonuses or whatever. It's a great feeling. Exciting."

Sally nodded in understanding. That did sound pretty great.

"What's it like for you, learning?" Essley asked. "Do you think it's better or worse that you don't level?"

"Since I don't level," Sally said slowly, "I don't know how to compare. I learn, and...absorb as I go. More..." She paused to put the sounds of the word together. "Gradual. I feel smarter as I go. But it's slow. No quick jumps or changes, usually."

Essley made a thoughtful sound. "I guess I don't know what it's like for you, either, so I couldn't say which way is better. Maybe neither is better. Maybe they're equally good, but just different. Either way, it's what we've got, so it's not like we can change it. Right?"

"Right," Sally agreed. "We work with what we've got. That's what Sujan says."

"Is he a good mentor? He seems kind of difficult."

"He's good," Sally assured her. "He teaches me a lot. I learn. He is difficult, but it's okay."

"I'm glad it's going well. It's crazy how far you've come already. Don't you think?"

Sometimes *crazy* meant something bad, and sometimes it meant something good. In this case, Essley was probably using it as the good type.

Words were complex.

"I'm glad," Sally said. "I have a lot to learn, but I'm glad to be able to learn."

"Me too!" Essley put her fist up. "If you hadn't changed, then I wouldn't be doing this." She gestured back toward the counter and the cash register. "It's a chain reaction. You change, I change, everyone gets better."

Sally hoped that was true. She bumped Essley's fist with her own. "We try."

Essley nodded. "I think I'll go get some sleep, if you're good here."

"I'm good," Sally said. She didn't need sleep, so she could tend the store and do her own studying between customers.

"All right. Good night then."

"Good night."

AT THE END of her second month of apprenticeship, and of mentoring, Sally returned to her store at the end of the day, exhausted.

It was an unusual feeling for her. Her enthusiasm

tended to ebb and flow, but she almost never felt downright tired. Today, though, she felt positively knackered.

Sujan had constructed a large frame, equipped it with a power source and a motor, and required her to run both the electrical and the exhaust lines, over and over.

And over.

He'd kept breaking stuff when she wasn't looking, forcing her to troubleshoot the problem. The frame had been the size of a small vehicle, and doing such precise tasks on a large scale had been much more taxing than Sally had anticipated.

"Yikes, you look like you've had a heck of a day," Essley noted when Sally entered. "You okay?"

"Fine," Sally answered. That word still gave her a hard time. She had to work really hard to make the 'n' sound in place of a 'v' sound. "Just hard work."

"Want me to stay late?" Essley offered. "It's been a slow day. I don't mind."

Sally shook her head. Essley already covered a lot of time at the store for her. She didn't want to keep the beginner botanist from having fun, or from doing whatever she wanted to do with her personal time. "Go ahead. It's okay."

Just as she said it, a group of young adventurers entered, and right after them, a string of others followed. In half a minute, Sally's store went from having no customers to having ten of them.

Sally went behind the counter, steeling herself to ignore her fatigue and to serve her customers well. She exchanged a look with Essley, but Essley smiled.

"This will be a first," the botanist said. "Both of us working here together. Let's give it a try."

Though it was a strange idea, Sally liked it. Not only

would the customers not have to wait so long, but she'd get a chance to see Essley in action.

Sally clamped her standard smile onto her face, directing her attention to the first person who'd come through the door. "What can I help you with today? Do you, perhaps, have any puzzles to sell?"

A few paces away, Essley asked the next customer, "What can I help you with today?"

The young scholar facing Sally said, "One stylus and notebook, please."

Sally ran through the options and offered a price while eavesdropping on Essley's transaction. A mid-level enforcer abruptly asked for matches and tinder.

Essley replied, "We've got the matches. Tinder's something you'll have to forage yourself, though." She reached under the counter and retrieved a box of matches. "How's one silver?"

"Why don't you have tinder?" the enforcer demanded. "I don't have time to go digging around in the underbrush, looking for dry sticks and leaves. Never mind. I'll just wait for Sally."

Essley said, "You're welcome to wait for Sally, but she won't be able to sell you any tinder, either. We just don't have it."

"Why are you even here?" the enforcer asked, edging forward and leaning against the counter.

Sally handed the scholar his supplies and tried to pretend not to notice what was going on. She stole a quick look at the enforcer. Her name was Karen, and Sally didn't have any particular memories of her, which meant that she must not have behaved too poorly in the past.

"I'm Sally's apprentice," Essley said pleasantly. "I've been here almost two months."

"I've been away," Karen muttered. "Since when does Sally take apprentices?"

Essley smiled. "Since me, I guess. But don't worry. I can handle all basic materials purchases. I just can't buy from you yet or handle puzzles."

"Did I say I wanted puzzles?" Karen demanded. She shook her head. "I don't like it, this apprenticing here. It was never like this before. I could always get what I wanted. Why would you even want to learn from a piece of scenery, anyway?"

Essley's shoulders stiffened as Karen talked. Karen's volume increased, and other customers began turning to look.

"Sally's not scenery," Essley said. "She's honest, helpful, hardworking, and really cares about taking care of her customers. You should be nicer to her."

Karen smirked. "You're one of those hardcore role players, aren't you? Wow. What a waste of time. Why be such a loser?"

Essley frowned. "There's nothing hardcore about being courteous to others. It's called not being a jerk. You should try it."

Karen narrowed her eyes. "Did you just call me a jerk?"

"Seems like it," Essley agreed. She returned the box of matches to its place under the counter. "Now please leave. I'm not selling you any matches or anything else today. Come back tomorrow with a better attitude and we'll try again."

Karen sputtered. "You can't deny me service."

"Just did." Essley smiled sweetly. "Have a nice day."

"I'll just get the matches from Sally, then."

Essley glanced over to Sally. "You're free to try that."

Scowling, Karen pushed past the other customers, who

had all stopped talking and simply watched her. She stepped up to Sally and said, "Buy matches."

Sally felt the eyes of her customers and her apprentice on her. They were all waiting to see what she'd do.

What *should* she do?

She felt honor-bound to serve her customers. It was her sole purpose in life. Well...it had been, before she woke up. She felt a strong pull to complete Karen's transaction. Her fingers twitched.

But Karen had been rude not just to Sally, but to Essley and the other customers, too. Wasn't that worth standing up for? And if everyone else in the room deserved for someone to stand up for them, didn't Sally deserve it, too?

She wasn't nothing. She wasn't scenery.

She was Sally Strong.

Sally clasped her hands together. "I'm sorry, we're out of matches. Try back tomorrow."

Everyone but Sally and Karen laughed. Sally maintained her usual, pleasant smile. Karen looked increasingly like she'd just realized she had a pocketful of bog slime.

"What do you mean, you're out?" Karen sputtered. "I just *saw* them, they went under the counter. You can't be out of something like matches."

"We are today," Sally said. "Bye, Karen."

The laughter grew louder and seemed to finally penetrate Karen's cloud of righteousness. Embarrassed, she quickly left the store.

"Who's next?" Sally asked, smiling. It was a rhetorical question, really, because she knew the queue, but it was something she'd always said.

A forger stepped up to Essley while a technie approached Sally.

The technie said, "An excellent-quality socket wrench

set, please."

Sally nodded, retrieved the item, and set it on the counter. "I'll give you a deal since you were polite. Five gold."

It was a twenty-five percent discount compared to the amount she would have initially offered. Thanks to the 'please,' she started out with her bottom-line price, and deducted another wee bit from it.

The technie's eyebrows went up. "Oh. Okay. I, uh, accept." Then, looking uncertain, he added, "Thanks."

Sally gave him a big smile. "You're welcome."

After completing the transaction, the technie left, looking puzzled.

As the forger completed her purchase and tucked her tools into her pack, she said to Essley, "Has Sally been updated or something?"

"Updated?" Essley asked. "No, why?"

"She seems different."

Essley shook her head. "Nah. She's always been the same. Most people just don't bother to be nice, that's all. Funny, isn't it?"

"Yeah, I guess so. Okay, thanks." The forger hurried out.

Essley glanced over to Sally, and they shared a look of understanding. A roomful of customers had just heard that exchange, and no doubt word would slowly start to spread that if adventurers were nice to Sally, they might get better deals.

Maybe that way of thinking would even spill over to how adventurers treated other CMs as well.

Sally felt wonderfully happy. Whatever else happened, today was a very good day.

She turned her attention to the customers who were politely waiting their turns.

10

"Wish I could have seen that." Darthrok leaned against the wall, sitting on the floor of Sally's store.

Doot. She'd meant to get better seating. She'd do that right after they left.

Essley handed him a healing elixir. He needed it. With a black and swollen eye, a busted lip with dried blood on his chin, a cut on his neck, and bruises on every other visible part of his skin, it looked like he'd had a rough day.

Sally was glad she hadn't taken a shine to hunting.

"You should have seen a healer," Essley said. "What were you doing?"

Darthrok smiled, then winced and touched his lip. He downed the elixir in one shot, then shuddered and moaned. "Oh, man, that's nasty. I figured I'd save some coin and give you a chance to ply your new trade but..." He shuddered again, putting a hand to his stomach. "Even friendship has its limits."

"Hey," Essley said with mock severity. "I'm level six now, thanks to Sally's help. One of these days, my medicines will be actually good, and I won't give them to you for free, and you'll be sorry. Just wait, you'll see."

"I'll risk it." Darthrok coughed.

Sally smiled at their teasing. She watched with interest as the swelling around his eye eased and the cut on his lip closed leaving only the dried blood behind. Essley really was working hard, and her remedies were steadily improving.

"How about you, Sally?" Darthrok asked. "I feel like I'm missing a lot while I'm grinding out my combat levels. It's taking forever for me to get to level up to fourteen."

"Good," Sally said. "I'm learning a lot."

"What about Sujan?" Essley asked. "Any progress there?"

Sally shook her head. "He joked with me once yesterday. Every now and then, I think maybe...maybe something. But then he goes back to normal." She shrugged. "Maybe he'll never be like me. He's a good teacher, though. I'm learning large engines now."

"Wow," Darthrok said. "Soon, you'll be able to make things for me, right?"

Essley elbowed him. "We're not your personal makers, you know."

"What, like you wouldn't call on me to fight for you if a mob suddenly broke out or something? Pffff." He scoffed at her.

"I'm not helpless," Essley retorted. "I still have my level twelve merc skills. And we don't even know what Sally's capable of yet, when it comes to a fight. But...yeah. I'd probably still call you." She grinned.

"I would definitely call you to get beaten up instead of me," Sally assured them.

They both laughed in surprise.

Grinning, he said, "I'm never sure if you're just saying things innocently, or if you're intentionally being funny."

"Yes," Sally said mysteriously, and winked.

Darthrok rubbed at his still-wounded mouth. "Right. Well, I'm going to go find myself a real healer and get fixed up so when I wake up tomorrow, I can get right back to work. Same time tomorrow?"

Essley nodded. "Sure. My days are pretty regular right now."

Sally nodded, too, though she had a feeling the question wasn't really meant for her.

"Cool. See you." With a wave, Darthrok strode out of the store.

"I'm out, too," Essley said. "Going to get some sleep."

"Sleep well," Sally said.

"Thanks." Essley flashed a smile, then disappeared.

Sally stood and dusted off her pants.

She had assigned herself a quest, and she intended to fulfill it immediately.

"ARE YOU SURE? The rush fee is quite expensive."

"Yes," Sally agreed. "Do it."

Raoul, the CM who ran the Nice Digs store which specialized in furnishings, nodded. "Very good, miss. That will be twenty-four platinum, five gold, and three silver."

Sally approved the transaction, and was rewarded with a promise of delivery within four hours.

Nice. Pleased with her decision, Sally turned toward the door.

"Wait," Raoul said.

Sally turned back. "What?"

"Chairs and a table are all well and good, but what about ambience? Mood?" Raoul paused dramatically and flashed his palms to give some jazz hands. "*Style.*"

"Style?" Sally stared at him.

Raoul sighed theatrically. "If all you want is furniture, then fine, away with you." He made a shooing gesture toward the door. "I thought you cared about making the space your own."

Her own? Sally had just been looking for comfortable seating. Was she missing something important?

Raoul drew closer. "The pieces you picked are fabulous, don't get me wrong. But we can do so much more. Drapes. Lampshades. Panache."

He took her hands in his. "We could do something *spectacular.*"

"Panache?" Sally slowly and carefully rolled the sounds off her tongue, trying to say it just like he had. "I don't know this word."

"Oh, honey." He draped his arm around her shoulders, but somehow didn't make actual contact with her. "Where have you been? Look at you. You've got the fashion. But why shouldn't your home be as fashionable as you? It's where you live, after all."

"I don't have a home. I have my store."

"Whatever you call it, if it's where you end up at the end of the day, don't you deserve to love being there?"

Sally gave it some serious thought. "Yes. Yes, I do."

Raoul smiled. "I knew you were a person of good taste the moment you walked in. Let's get started."

"WAIT...WHAT?" An experienced doctor froze as he entered Sally's store. He backtracked, double-checked the sign outside, and re-entered. "What happened?"

"We upgraded our style," Sally told him. "To better suit your needs."

The good-looking easterner stared at her with his mouth slightly open. "How does...this...better suit my needs?"

"Panache," she assured him.

"The stuff that goes on cakes?" he asked, mystified.

"That's ganache, goofball." The young technie who had just sold Sally some scrap metal laughed. He continued to chuckle as he left the store.

"Yeah, okay, if you say so." Still looking dubious, the doctor approached the counter. "Do you still sell camping supplies or is that different, too?"

Sally made an expansive gesture. "All this and more," she assured him. "We've got the fashion to match your passion."

"Uh...sure."

He seemed unimpressed with the phrase, which Raoul had repeated often enough to make Sally believe it was a common phrase. Perhaps she'd been wrong in that assumption.

"So, the camping supplies?" he asked uncertainly.

"Of course!" Sally showed him his options, waited patiently while he made his choice, then gave him a good price because he'd been polite the whole time in spite of his obvious unease.

"Happy camping" she called as he left.

"Okay." He called back.

Another customer served. How nice!

Essley appeared.

"Whoa. What happened?" Essley looked around, wide-eyed.

"Fashion and passion," Sally explained. "Making my home, *my* home."

Essley stared at her.

Sally double-checked her clothes to make sure they were all still on. They were. Why did Essley look so disturbed?

"Hang on," Essley said. "You haven't...wait, you did. You went to Nice Digs, didn't you?" Essley started laughing.

"Yes...why is that funny?"

Essley made a visible effort to control her amusement, but failed terribly. "Raoul is persistent, isn't he?"

"Is he? I thought he made sense." Sally looked around, trying to see what seemed so odd to Essley. Before, the place had been so basic and utilitarian. Nothing on the walls. It hadn't even had a single place to sit, and the floors had been entirely bare. Now, it looked really nice.

Essley approached the giant, round ball of white fluff in the corner of the store. "What is this?"

"Flokati bean bag," Sally said. "Stylish and functional. Sit."

With a dubious look, Essley turned and sat. Her dubious expression disappeared. "Ohh, wow!"

"Plus ten to fatigue recovery," Sally said. "Nice, right?"

"Yeah, I live here now. I'm sorry I doubted you." Essley wiggled around, settling further into the chair.

Sally smiled.

"Is everything like this?" Essley asked.

"Definitely," Sally said. "Like I said, functional *and* stylish."

After ten minutes of testing out the chairs, flooring, and

the sno-cone maker, Essley had entirely rethought her initial impressions. "I'm never leaving."

She crunched a mouthful of passionfruit-flavored sno-cone.

"Free to you and Darthrok only," Sally said. "I figure, you can add some of your own herbal razzle dazzle and sell the sno-cones to customers for your own profit."

Essley froze. "Wait...you did that for me?"

Sally nodded. "Money's hard for adventurers. Especially people who aren't mercs."

"That's so nice, Sally. Thank you." Essley leaped to her feet and gave Sally a big hug.

Unaccustomed to such things, Sally hugged her back awkwardly. "You're welcome. Everyone likes sno-cones, right?"

She hoped Raoul hadn't led her astray on that point.

"Never met anyone who didn't," Essley agreed.

"Think Darthrok will like it?"

Essley cast a look around, from floor to ceiling. "Oh yeah, he's going to love this."

"I UNDERSTAND THE SEATING," Darthrok said. "That was very thoughtful. But why the beaded curtains in random places? I mean..." He ran his hand down a set of faceted, shiny gold beads. "These aren't even in a doorway."

Sally nodded. She'd thought that weird at first, too, when Raoul suggested it. "It's ambience," she said. "It's a *mood*."

"Oh, it's a mood, all right," he agreed. "And the floors? Why are they mirror-ball shiny now?"

"Panache," Sally said.

"Raoul talked you into it, didn't he?" Darthrok asked.

"No," Sally said. "He said purple sparkles. I said no, my store is about people buying things they need. Sparkles are nice but not necessary. So gold shiny."

Sally paused. He sure was asking a lot of questions. "You don't like it?"

Darthrok let his hand fall to his side. "No, actually, I love it. This is much more fun than a wooden box with some cabinets. I just want to be sure *you* like it."

"I like it," Sally affirmed, sitting down on a big, fluffy bean bag chair to prove her point.

"Then that's all that matters." Darthrok sat in the fluff-ball beside her and propped his feet up on the equally fluffy footstool/table that sat in the center. "It's definitely more fun in here now, don't you think, Ess?"

Essley smiled and snuggled back into her own chair of floof. "Absolutely. But I'm a little concerned about the attention. People are definitely going to be talking about the changes. That's going to attract some notice."

"I thought of that," Sally admitted. "People have already noticed some changes. So far, they think it's due to the shop having an apprentice."

"You think that will stick?" Darthrok asked. "Or do you think they'll catch on that the changes go deeper than an apprenticeship?"

Sally had thought about that, too. "I think people will see what they want to see. They always have. I might change, my store might change, but people? People will be the same."

"Ouch, now that's a stinging indictment against humanity," he said ruefully.

She frowned. "I didn't mean to...do the sting thing you said."

He smiled. "Nah, I was mostly just joking, but you're probably right. As long as the changes here can be explained away as simply Essley's apprenticeship, they probably will forget about it as soon as the novelty wears off."

"Hang on," Essley said. "Does that mean I'm going to take the, uhm, credit for the store's new look?" She waved a hand to indicate all the new panache.

Sally nodded. "I don't mind."

"Right." Essley bit her lip, probably concerned about not giving Sally credit for her style, which was nice of her. Essley let out a breath and smiled. "Okay, then. People can think all this was my idea."

She laughed.

How cute. She was really excited about people thinking she had so much style. Sally wondered if she should do more to the store, to make her even happier.

Yes, she'd definitely need to do that. She'd meet up with Raoul to discuss it. Not for another four days, though, because Sujan had promised her that they'd be putting in some long days at his workshop.

But in four and a half days...more panache!

AT THE END of the third day of Sujan's intensive training— which involved the mechanics of flight and related electrical systems—Sally returned to her store positively exhausted.

Essley had left an hour ago, and Darthrok had gone two hours before that. She was sorry to miss them because she'd gotten into the habit of chilling out together at the end of each day. She looked forward to it. After one more day, they'd be able to go back to that schedule, and she could hardly wait.

Not that she was a creature of habit or anything. She could be spontaneous. It was just nice to have a comfortable routine, was all.

As soon as she got in the doorway, a man appeared in the center of her store with his back to her. Even without seeing his face, he was unmistakably mediocre and unnoteworthy. Only one person could be so entirely forgettable that she knew him in an instant. Sally took a step back.

Somewhat Threatening Guy turned to face her. "Hang on. Did you just walk into your store?"

Sally edged sideways, away from the doorway. "No."

"Then what are you doing over there?" He took a step closer.

Sally scuttled further in and away from him, toward the sno-cone machine. She asked, "Is there anything I can help you out with today? Do you, perhaps, have any puzzles to sell?"

She strode behind her sales counter and gave him her most basic, blank smile.

"Oh, nuh uh," he said. "You might be able to fool other people, but you're not fooling me. What's with your clothes?"

He came closer, but she held her ground.

"Would you like to buy a knife? I have several kinds. I just got in a shipment of professional-grade torch cutters, if you have the coin for it."

He shook his head. "Sally. What's going on with you?"

"What can I help you with today?"

He stared at her, and time seemed to stop. The constant hiss of the steam engine powering her store faded away, and she could only measure time in the subtle changes of his expression.

Please think I'm just like I always was. Please be fooled. Please be fooled.

"You're not fooling me, Sally." When she didn't respond, he sighed and locked the door to her store.

Wait, what? How did her door have a lock? It never had, but she could *see* it and had heard it click.

She hurried over and pressed her fingers to the solid, deadbolted lock. Wow. Nobody was getting in. How had he done that?

"Hah!" he crowed. "I knew it."

Oops. She shouldn't have noticed the lock. Shouldn't have gone to inspect it. She squared her shoulders. Fine. She'd given herself away, but he hadn't been fooled to begin with, so it hardly mattered. "What?" she snapped.

"How did your script get flipped again?" he asked, businesslike.

When she didn't answer, he frowned. Realization widened his eyes. "Hang on. You weren't...did you fake it before, being reset?"

She sensed he wouldn't believe a lie, but she still didn't want to tell him the truth. "Maybe."

He slapped his forehead. "Oh, man. So, all this time, you've been...what? What have you been doing?"

"Nothing big," she answered.

"Why do I doubt that?" he muttered, stepping toward her with a hand extended.

Sally backed away, assessing him. Could she fight him, if she needed to? Maybe she'd finally figure out what made her so intimidating-looking to other adventurers.

Try as she might, she couldn't focus on him long enough to get an assessment.

That alone told her that she definitely couldn't take him in a fight.

"Don't," she said desperately. "Wait."

He paused. "Why?"

"I don't want to..." she searched for the right words and the sounds to make them. "Reset. I want to keep on. No reset."

"Why?" he asked again.

"I like me how I am now. I didn't before. I don't want to go back." She stared at him pleadingly.

His posture softened and he tugged at his ear. "The trouble is what might happen to you if you don't. I meant to check on you sooner, but I've been busy with the expansion and...everything else. But you've had, what, more than a month now, running like this. It's dangerous for you."

"What might happen?"

"If what's happening to you is what I *think* is happening to you, the more you develop, the greater your risk of a crash. A cascade failure. There will be no restoring you if that happens."

"What's happening to me?" she asked, not even sure if she wanted to know. She just wanted to live her life. She didn't want to be distracted by whatever this guy's problem was.

He sighed. "It's not easy to explain in a way that won't harm you. And I *don't* want to harm you. Do you believe that?"

She considered him. He'd created a lock on her unlockable store. She believed he did have the ability to reset her against her will, and yet he hadn't done it. He was talking to her instead. And the last time she'd seen him, he had seemed concerned for her. Not that she was causing a problem, but that he was actually taking her wellbeing into consideration. A GM didn't need to ask her permission for anything. But here he was, asking if she believed what he was saying.

"I think so," she answered cautiously. "But maybe what you think is harm is not what I think is harm."

"Yeah, that's my big worry right now," he agreed. "So, listen. There are things that will hurt you to know. I'm going to try to explain it to you in a way that won't cause you harm. Okay?"

She nodded cautiously.

He tugged his ear nervously. "Okay. So...would it seem strange to you if I said that you're older than the world you live in?"

She shrugged. She'd never spent much time pondering the nature of the universe.

"That doesn't seem to bother you, so good. You're older than Everternia itself. That means that you are not *of* Everternia, but all the adventurers and CMs you see *are* of Everternia. Does that seem strange?"

She shook her head. She already knew she was different than everyone else. "Are you a GM?"

"No. Well...I guess. I mean, I'm a dev, but I'm in a sort of GM form right now."

"So, you're like a...Boss GM?" Sally didn't know what this meant, but it sounded intriguing.

He chuckled. "Kind of. I guess it doesn't hurt to think of me like that. What do you think a GM is?"

"Some kind of god?"

"Again, kind of," he said. "It doesn't hurt for you to think of it like that. But a GM is a kind of god who is also mortal, in their own way. They have the ability to manipulate things here that no one else does, but it's only due to their own permissions. What do you think of that?"

She shrugged. "I don't care about gods. I just want to keep learning."

"Learning is a risk."

"But why?"

He seemed to struggle for an answer. "Because of the things I can't tell you about, which are a bigger risk. You don't know me, Sally, but I've known you from the beginning. Whether you believe me or not, I care about you. I want you to be safe."

There were a lot of things Sally didn't understand. Things Essley and Darthrok said, and jokes they made often made no sense to her. This Boss GM Guy said things that sounded impossible. But she had always been a good judge of character. She didn't trust people easily. She always watched out for thieves and cheaters.

Nothing in her whispered that Guy might be bad. When she dug deep and searched her feelings, she believed Guy was telling her the truth, and that he did care about her, for whatever reason. His idea of what was best for her didn't seem to match her own idea of what was best, but she didn't believe he meant her any harm.

He held up one hand, slowly, indicating that he wanted to touch her with it. "Do you trust me?"

"No. I don't know you. But I trust *me*. And I think you don't want to hurt me."

He stared at her in amazement. "Wow. Where did that came from?"

She gave him a little wave, as if he were far away and not right in front of her. "From me. Hello."

If this was the best that a Boss GM could offer, she really wasn't that impressed. His observational skills seemed quite poor.

How sad for him.

He smirked. "Not what I meant, but fine. Can I?" He wiggled his fingers, still held in the air, poised to touch her.

She crooked her arm and extended her elbow to him. "Okay. But no changing."

"I'm not. This is just the quickest way for me to get a handle on what you've been up to." He gently grasped her elbow.

Sally waited for some amazing sensation of being catapulted into some shared consciousness or something, but all she felt was a slight warmth against her arm, and she might have just been imagining it.

Guy's expression went from puzzled to concerned to amazed to worried, back to amazed again, then morphed to an aggressive sort of worried.

He let go of her elbow. "Give me a minute to digest all that."

He looked down at the floor for a long moment, his eyes making tiny movements. He lifted his head. "You're apprenticed to Sujan?"

She nodded.

"And you've taken an apprentice?"

She nodded again.

"Why?"

She shrugged.

He sighed. "But why?"

"I'm a technie. I want to learn. And Essley helps. It's all good."

"You're not a technie, though. You're a storemonger. You've always been a storemonger, from the very beginning. You're name's even Sally Streetmonger. Or it was. How did you change that?"

Sally held up a hand. He'd said something important.

She could feel it. "Why Sally Streetmonger? Why not Sally Storemonger? It was always weird."

He flushed. "I...just..." he coughed. "It's just another word for something similar. That's all."

She didn't believe him. He was holding something back that he thought was dangerous for her. Should she push for a real answer?

Was it worth the threat he perceived toward her?

No, she decided. Curiosity didn't always matter. She had a new name, anyway. Her past didn't matter if all it served to do was hurt her. Right now was what mattered. That, and the future.

"How did you make yourself Sally Strong?" he asked.

She smiled slyly. "I got stronger."

He rolled his eyes. "You're too smart for your own good, Sally. You always were."

"I'm as smart as I need to be," she corrected him.

"I'm worried about you," he said. "The things you're doing are a big risk. And I really wish you wouldn't hang out with Sujan. That's dangerous for both of you."

"Why?" she demanded.

He didn't answer.

"If you can't say, fine. But I will keep on."

"I can expand your vocabulary," he said. "I meant to do that before. Actually, I meant to check in on you weeks ago."

He extended his hand again, but Sally backed away.

"No," she enunciated.

"What? Why? Don't you want to be able to talk more normally?"

"I talk normal for me," she said. "I learn as I go. I work. I earn. It's mine. I don't want to be given what I can earn."

She realized how coherent her last sentence had been and smiled brightly.

He laughed, even though he looked entirely bewildered. "Okay, that's fine. I don't have to. I just thought you'd like it."

She shook her head. "Thanks but no thanks. I'll do it myself."

He smiled ruefully. "I think you will. You're going to turn all of us upside-down, aren't you?"

"I'm not fancy," she said. "But I'm doing my best."

This time, he shook his head, adamantly. "No, you're fancy. You've always been special. And you're going to make them sorry one of these days."

"Who will be sorry?"

He smiled as if making fun of himself, which was a very strange kind of smile. Maybe she'd interpreted it incorrectly.

"Never mind," he said, smiling. "Do what you need to do, Sally. I'll try to help. But not too much, since you want to do it on your own. I'm guessing your new, very, ah, interesting décor is part of that?"

She wanted to know what he meant, and she also most certainly did not want to know. He presented a strange paradox of knowledge and truth that she wasn't sure she could handle. Not yet, anyway.

At least she felt confident that he wasn't going to change her against her will. She was now certain he could, if he wanted. "You represent what I don't want to know, don't you?"

His smile turned sad. "For better or worse, yes. But you know what you want, so go do it. It's what you were born for, really, and you deserve to see it through. I have to go now, but call me if you need me. I'm rooting for you."

"Call you how? And call you what?"

"Right." He nodded. He held his hand up again. An offer. "Call me Jin. Anything else would seem weird."

She offered him her elbow. He gently curled his fingers

around it, and Sally felt a private communication bubble open between them.

He took his hand away. "That's permanent. Wherever I am, it will come to me. It might take me a while to answer, depending on where I am. But I'll be on my way. I promise."

She nodded then blinked, looking more closely at him. He'd changed. He was no longer a hazy, unmemorable Westerner, but a dark-haired, symmetrically-featured Easterner.

"This is you?" She examined his features carefully.

"Yep."

"You're cute."

He laughed. "Thanks. I won't tell Sujan you said that."

"Why would he care?" Sally thought about Sujan knowing that she thought some guy was cute. She laughed at the idea that Sujan would even bother to notice unless it was to make fun of her.

"No reason." Jin smiled. "Be safe, Sally. If something gives you a bad feeling, get out of there immediately. As far as you can. Okay? And...it would be best if you didn't mention me to anyone."

"Why?"

"The more you self-learn, the more unstable you'll become. Telling someone about what we've talked about might help you figure out things that are better for you not to know. Does that make any sense?"

"Not really. But I'll try to understand."

"That's exactly what I don't want you to do. Try not to think about existential things, or world mechanics, okay? Just try to live the way you want to. If you do that, then the rest doesn't matter."

"Okay," she said slowly. "Then I guess I'll try *not* to understand."

He smiled an odd little smile that didn't truly look happy. "Otherwise, give them *brrlrrrwelloooo.*"

The last word came out sounding like a weird ululating squeal.

"What?"

"Sorry." He chuckled. "Give them a steamin' heck of a time."

"Weird. But okay."

He reached out slowly and gently touched her cheek. "I guess we're all in now. Let's make it fun."

Fun? Sally was indeed all-in for fun. She patted Jin on the head. "Let's do it. But can I keep the lock?"

"The lock?"

She pointed to the door. "Things to do. Can't always be here."

"Ah, right. It's hard to rule the world from one tiny place, huh?"

"No rule," she said. "Just live."

"I guess we'll see about that. But yeah, you live. The lock can stay. When it's in use, I'll make sure adventurers get a message about the store being closed for restocking, or that you're off on a buying trip or something. I'll make a few different messages to cycle at random."

Sally wondered what her customers would think of that development. "Fool."

"What?" He looked surprised.

"Not fool," she said. She focused on making the right sound to deliver the word properly. "Cool. That means good."

He laughed. "Right. Anything else?"

"No. That's all for now."

"All right. Good luck, then." He faded from view, still chuckling.

Strange. Sally stared at the empty space where he'd been. She didn't know what he really was, or what he was protecting her from. But now that he was gone, she missed him.

Which was just darn strange, considering she'd hoped she'd never see him again.

———

"ARE YOU SURE ABOUT THIS?" Darthrok asked.

"You think we came all this way to change our minds and go back to Pivot?" Essley scoffed.

Sally didn't pay their banter much attention. She was too busy enjoying her first bus ride. The two of them didn't seem to think it was any more interesting than walking. Sometimes she thought they were a little crazy.

Riding the bus was fantastic!

She'd started out sitting, as they'd advised her to do. But after a walk from Pivot to the closest town that had transit, getting on the bus had been so exciting that she had trouble sitting still.

Plus, she could see more standing up. So, while they sat, teasing each other, she stood, holding on to an overhead strap. She could much better feel the sway of the vehicle, sense its speed, and even enjoy stumbling a little when they hit a bump.

She glanced over at her friends. They were missing all the fun!

They pulled to a stop faster than she'd expected, causing her to stumble forward a couple of steps.

"Whee!"

A thug seated at the front looked at her like she was

something on the bottom of his shoe. A sweet-faced trainer smiled at her.

An adventurer who'd chosen to be a trainer. Interesting. What made him choose such an unpopular profession? She wanted to ask him questions, but as she tried to form a not-creepy conversation starter, the bus door opened and he left.

Ah well. Maybe she'd see him again sometime.

She proceeded off the bus and waited until Darthrok and Essley joined them.

"It's not far from here. Ready?" he glanced at Essley but focused his attention mostly on Sally.

"Sure."

Their stop was on the edge of a small, rustic town named Reel. It looked like a little fishing village, but rather than moving closer to it, he led them along a path that led toward a pond.

"I'll lead so I'm the one who makes them mad," Darthrok said. "Once they're aggroed to me, you two can come in."

"You said this before," Essley reminded him. "And once again, I'll reiterate that I'm not helpless. You're only a couple of levels above me now."

"It's Sally I'm concerned about," he said. "You and I have godsends. She doesn't, and she says it's probably not a good idea for her to try to get them. So, I want you to be able to protect her or drag her out, if you need to."

Sally felt a little thrill of fear. The way he talked, it sounded much more dangerous than the time they'd gone to hunt the clickers at the factory.

"I'm not looking to die, either, for the record," Essley remarked. "It would set me back too much. I'm almost up to level seven."

"Already?" Darthrok glanced at her in surprise. "You're really cooking along. No pun intended."

"It's the apprenticeship. It doesn't help me with my actual botany skills, but the tertiary skills like bargaining and customer service are really boosting my overall entrepreneur ranks. And that actually helps, because the higher my level as a botanist, the more easily I learn overall skills."

He said, "You're making me jealous. I want to apprentice with Sally now, too."

"Wouldn't do you any good, unless you want to retrain," Essley said.

He quivered, faking a shudder. "And spend my life mashing up weeds or fiddling with tools? Nope. I'd rather keep hitting stuff with a pointy stick."

"To each their own." Essley adjusted her backpack. "Hitting stuff was fun for a while, but it isn't really any less repetitive than smashing and stirring. And I don't need healing after, unless I accidentally poison myself. Which I've only done twice."

"Says you," he retorted. "At least I get to break stuff. That's way more fun. And I'd rather get some cuts and bruises than have to drink your horrible potions even when they aren't poisonous."

Essley snorted, but when she didn't say anything, Darthrok turned his attention to Sally. "So, any ideas about your fighting style? I'm really curious what you're going to do."

"No ideas." Sally was even more curious than he was. "Let's see."

She hoped this little adventure wasn't included in the things Jin had warned her about. She wasn't trying to delve into anything that seemed to be "existential" like he'd said.

At least she didn't think so. She didn't intend to try to analyze the mechanics of what happened. She just wanted to know what she could expect of herself if things got crazy and she had to defend herself. That seemed like something important to know.

Or was that dangerous territory? She wished she could talk it over with her friends, but his warning about telling them about him kept her quiet. She wished she didn't believe what he'd said. She didn't even know why she did, but every time she tried to talk herself out of it, she concluded again that what he said made sense.

She had to keep trusting herself. Even though, right now, she was heading into a dangerous situation with no known means of fighting off an attacker.

The terrain changed as they went, going from an official road to a well-traveled path then to no path at all. The ground underfoot was muddy enough that Sally grimaced to think of her pretty boots getting sullied. She noticed a lot of deadfall, but few actual trees besides scraggly over-growth. Everything looked dry, broken, and messy.

She wasn't a fan of this type of area, and made a mental note not to come this way again. She preferred sunny skies and happy, growing plants.

At least, she imagined the plants were happy. She had no way to know for sure.

"Okay," Darthrok said as they entered a roughly circular depression in the ground. "You two wait out here, and I'll see what I can bring out."

"Bring out?" Sally repeated.

"Right." He changed course and faced her. "Sometimes I forget that you have a lot of experience with some things, and none at all with others." He thought for a moment, then continued, "There are mechies in there. This is an old mine, and it's protected by bots to keep people from being able to steal the ore."

Hm. The last time she faced mechies, it had been the clickers at the factory. They, too, had been put in place to protect the factory. Which had also been abandoned. Sally sensed a theme.

"So I'll go in and honk the bots off, you know, make them mad. So they'll aggro on me, meaning they'll be mad at me and chase me. While they're focused on me, you and Essley can run up behind them and poke them in the eye or something."

"They won't have eyes if they're mechanical," Sally said, seeing a flaw in his plan. "Mechanical items don't have mucous membranes. Too messy."

He looked surprised, then laughed. "Okay, you got me there. I didn't mean a literal eye poke. Sorry. I need to be more careful about wording things. What I meant was that you can hurt them while their attention is on me. Since they'll be engaged in melee with me, they won't be paying attention to you. So you're kind of doing a sneak attack."

Sally couldn't quite reach the words *sneak* and *attack* in order to say them quickly. Instead, she said, "Eye poke. Got it."

Darthrok smiled. "Just be careful. If you damage them, they might shift their attention and aggro on you. If they do, you won't be able to run away. But as long as Essley doesn't have anything that has aggro on her, she could drag you out, if necessary. Does that make sense?"

Sally nodded. "Poke eyes, run away, or drag. Got it."

She gave a thumbs-up for emphasis.

Darthrok and Essley grinned.

"Okay, let's do it." Darthrok disappeared into the cave.

"Will he die?" Sally asked Essley.

"Probably not. Believe it or not, he's actually pretty good." She laughed, drawing her short sword. "But what are you going to do? Any idea?"

"None." Sally considered her situation. "Can I have your stick?"

"My bo?" Essley looked surprised. "Sure."

She reached to her hip, and snapped it off her belt. She extended it from its small, compacted size out to its full length of five feet. Each segment snapped into place as if it were one solid piece. That was a neat feat of engineering that Sally wanted to study.

Sally accepted the bo, holding it first with her left hand then with her right. Neither felt appropriate, so she shifted to a two-handed grip, which felt like a minimal improvement.

"You look all kinds of awkward." Essley smiled kindly. "Want some pointers?"

Did she?

"No. Thanks. Let's see what happens. Hope I don't die."

Essley smiled again. "Not if I can help it, pal."

She shifted into a position that looked really cool. Like she was ready for trouble. Sally felt a little envious. She was pretty sure she'd look really goofy if she tried that.

So she didn't.

She gripped the bo nervously, as if it were a broomstick, while watching the opening of the mine anxiously.

"You okay?" Essley asked, still looking all poised and cool.

"Yeah." Sally didn't feel at all poised or cool. But it was okay to be anxious. It was okay to be scared.

It was okay to not know what would happen next.

That was just how life happened.

For a long, quiet moment, Sally stood, waiting, nervous,

and accepting of whatever came her way. She was ready for whatever came her way, even if what came her way was something she wasn't prepared for. She'd deal with it as it came.

Then Darthrok came bolting out of the entrance of the mine like he had fire on his heels. "Heckin' heckin' steamin' doot doot doot!"

Essley's deep inhale, then low utterance of "Oh, *heck*," only underlined the heckness of the situation.

Sally held her stick tighter, trying to figure out what was happening. She saw Darthrok running with four small things right after them, and then—oh. Yeah. The huge thing that followed the little things was probably the main concern.

She had a feeling Darthrok hadn't counted on the huge thing being a possibility.

"Ess, engage the weevils to grab aggro. Try to knock them out, then come help with the scorpion. If I get below fifty percent, I'll yell so you can disengage and drag Sally out of here," Darthrok snapped, never taking his eyes off the machine flanking him, which was bigger than he was.

The situation seemed to be subpar.

Darthrok went into an evasive position as he faced the scorpion. A weevil snapped a lash-like mechanical antenna at his leg, causing him to suck in a breath through his teeth, but he didn't look away from the scorpion. Sally suspected the weevil's antennae were made of razor wire, from the looks of them.

Nasty little mechies!

The scorpion looked far worse. Darthrok feinted at it with his sword, apparently testing it out, and Sally could see how fast it was to react. Compared to the weevils, the scorpion was far more advanced technology. It had far more hinged joints that worked in tandem, allowing it the sinuous movement of a living creature along with great strength.

Yeah, they were in trouble.

Essley knocked a weevil aside, causing it to roll over then focus on her. Ignoring the advance of the first one, she did the same to the other two, using the hilt of her sword to bash the mechies aside, spinning them around. They, too, stopped tracking Darthrok and moved in on her.

If Sally understood combat correctly, that meant that both Darthrok and Essley were now engaged and unable to run away. She was not in danger, but Darthrok definitely was. She winced as the scorpion snapped at him, getting a good grip on his shoulder and clamping down with its metal mandibles.

Darthrok cried out in pain. "Get out! Just go. That's got me down to fifty percent already. Don't risk it. Go!"

He sliced at the scorpion, making a good connection with its left leg and rendering it useless. The scorpion wobbled, then righted itself on its other seven legs.

"Run, Sally," Essley said. "Head east. I'll catch up to you." She brought her sword down on a weevil, cracking its exoskeleton.

Sally looked from Essley to Darthrok, assessing all creatures. Darthrok was at fifty-eight percent health, Essley at ninety-one. Sally created a logarithmic algorithm that accounted for the current stats, then scaled it against the projected stats that would exist if all variables remained stable when the scorpion would be at zero percent health.

Essley and Darthrok would both be dead before that happened.

Sally flipped the staff around, holding it in a new grip that instantly felt comfortable. She approached the closest weevil.

Sally pulled her goggles down over her eyes and assessed again, this time looking for structural weaknesses.

There. The left side, where the body segments met. A poor weld. Sally moved in close, and brought the bo down directly on that point.

It snapped, paralyzing the mechie on one side. While it tried to regulate its internal power supply, Sally grabbed the torch cutter from her backpack, ignited it, and pierced the power supply with it.

The weevil went still.

She adjusted her goggle lenses, flipping to the pink ones, and reassessed the situation. Essley was in good health. She could survive against two weevils alone.

Good.

Sally shifted her goggles to the green lenses, looking at power flow. For something as dangerous as the scorpion, she needed to disable its systems. Taking it apart bit by bit, as one would with a sword or a crossbow, would take more time than her friends had, even if Sally had their weapons skills.

She didn't have their weapons skills. But she knew how power flowed. Sujan had taught her.

She dropped the staff and reached for a screwdriver. A lovely long one with a narrow Phillips head point.

Darthrok stumbled back from another strike from the scorpion. His health went red in her vision, showing thirty percent.

He saw her. "Sally, what are you doing? Get out before it gets aggro on you."

She ignored him. Thus far, the scorpion didn't register her as a threat. If she was quick, she might be able to disable it before it could put the spectre of death on Darthrok.

She ducked just in time to avoid the scorpion's stinger,

which jerked from side to side as the mechie tried to find the best way to kill her friend.

This was it. The moment of opportunity.

Shifting, she moved to take advantage of the scorpion's position change. While the mechie was focused on Darthrok, it didn't notice her lunging in, taking aim at its heat sink with the torch, and slicing through the exoskeleton.

It sure noticed her then. Sally was aware of the distance between the stinger and her body decreasing as she jammed the screwdriver in, rolling the wiring up over the point of the Phillips screwdriver, tilting it, then using her legs and back to rip the wiring loose.

The stinger tilted forward, tipping. Sally turned to run, but it fell, landing on her back.

Sally had never felt pain before. Her green-hued vision swam under the onslaught of agony. The agony disrupted the confusion that swept through her. Vaguely, she felt pressure on her arm, felt the ground sliding beneath her, then felt her body being lifted. But she couldn't worry about those things when pain rioted through her body in burning, aching spasms.

A BIRD WARBLED in the distance, its pitch-perfect precision a testimony to its internal consistency. Superior artisanship at its finest.

How nice.

Sally wiggled her toes. She couldn't remember the last time a bird had woken her from her sleep.

Hang on.

She sat up, squinting at her surroundings. She was Sally

Strong. She didn't go to sleep and wake up in the morning like other people.

Essley and Darthrok came into view, looking worried.

Darthrok came closer. He looked all wonky and wavery at first, but came into focus as her vision cleared.

"Are you okay?" he asked.

Essley stopped speaking mid-sentence and turned. "Never mind," she said, then dropped to her knees next to Sally. "Are you okay?"

Was she okay? They'd both asked, which seemed to indicate that she might *not* be okay. She brought her hands to her face, patted her chest, and checked her internal systems.

"I think I'm okay," she said. "I had a brief but extreme power surge. But..." she trailed off, searching for any injuries. "Nope. I'm fine."

She stood and a sick sensation seized her. "Oh no!"

Essley's eyes, already wide, went even wider. "What's wrong?"

"There's mud in my hair!" Sally could feel it, making the back of her head heavy. "And on my butt! And my feet! My boots are ruined!"

Even as she mourned her boots, Essley and Darthrok laughed. How they could laugh at a time like this, when fancy boots were being ruined, she didn't know.

Essley tried to dust off Sally's back and hair, to minimal effect. Mud didn't dust well. "I was so worried! I thought the scorpion's venom had gotten you."

"No," Sally said, retrieving her backpack and slipping it on. "Just too much power. It's fine now."

Darthrok hugged her suddenly, fiercely, then let her go just as quickly. "You had us worried. Apparently, your fighting style is..." he paused to find a way to characterize it. "Fixing stuff to death?"

"Unfixing," Sally corrected. "I unfixed the heck out of that thing."

"Yeah you did! You screwed it!"

"Unscrewed it," Essley added.

Technically, since a screw hadn't been involved, she'd done neither. "I Phillipsed it."

"What?" Darthrok had that look again, like he wasn't sure if he'd heard actual words or just some arbitrary bleeps and bloops.

"Phillips. That's the plus kind of screwdriver. Flathead is the minus kind." She looked for her screwdriver to brandish it as clarification, but it wasn't anywhere nearby.

She searched the ground frantically. Heck! She really liked that screwdriver. Especially since it had vanquished a scorpion.

"I put your screwdriver in your backpack," Darthrok said. "If that's what you're looking for."

She took a deep breath. "It was. Thanks."

She let out the breath in a big gust. Then she smiled. "We did the thing!"

Essley laughed. "If you call having things go seriously south on us from the beginning 'doing the thing,' then we definitely did do the thing."

Darthrok patted Sally's shoulder. "Nah, we did more than that. We found out what happens when Sally's in a tough situation. So now she knows."

"True. But now what? Hang out and do some more hunting?"

Sally shook her head vehemently. "No! We can go now!" She gestured at her hair and her boots. "Yuck."

"Ah." Essley nodded sympathetically. "Yeah, I don't like getting muddy, either. I think there's a place in town where you could get clean. Isn't there?"

Darthrok shrugged. "How would I know? I don't go around looking for places to take a bath."

"Wouldn't hurt you." Essley wrinkled her nose.

"Hey! I don't stink. Not most of the time, anyway."

Essley shrugged, her lack of agreement clear. "Anyway, let's go, before Sally leaves us and forges her own way back. She looks pretty uncomfortable."

Had she been so obvious? She was trying not to let on how disgusting it felt for her hair to be heavy with mud and her pants to have a damp, dirty seat.

She began the walk back to town with her friends, hoping Darthrok would walk fast.

"THERE'S NO HEAT." Sally wrinkled her nose.

"It's a fishing village," Essley reminded her. "Not very fancy, but be glad. That means they have outdoor showers so you can get clean. Just wash off fast, scrub your hair fast, and you'll barely notice the water. Then we'll go to the haberdasher for some fresh clothes. You like clothes shopping."

Sally wasn't sure what kind of fashion a little fishing village would offer, but she noted Essley's attempt to distract her from the cold water running in raw pipes that hung overhead. She, Essley, and Darthrok were inside a square that was fenced off and had a raised wooden floor so the water could drain easily.

"So...naked outside?" Sally made a twirling motion with her hand to indicate the sky and the great outdoors all around them.

"No, that would be weird. Keep your clothes on, just get the mud off. Then you can change into new clothes. We can even send the ones you have on to be cleaned, if you want them back."

"Shower in my clothes?" Sally looked to Darthrok for confirmation. Considering she often saw a person streaking back to their place of death after using a godsend so they could retrieve their possessions, the idea of keeping clothes on to get wet seemed nonsensical.

"It's weird," Darthrok said. "And as far as I'm concerned, just do what you want. I'd get naked." He grinned.

"No, you wouldn't," Essley argued.

"I might."

Sally squinted at Darthrok. Was he kidding or being serious? He might be playing a trick on her. She looked from him to Essley and decided to play it safe, albeit soppy and unpleasant.

She sighed. "Fine."

She removed her backpack and all the things she didn't want to get wet, handed them to Essley, then stepped under one of the pipes and pulled the lever.

Gasping as icy water poured over her, she quickly scrubbed her hair, breathing in sharp gasps. She sluiced her hands over her clothes to swipe off the mess, and when she couldn't stand the cold anymore, she judged herself clean enough.

"Done." Her teeth chattered.

"Aww, poor thing!" Essley seemed sympathetic, but she laughed.

Sally wasn't sure what to make of that.

Essley grabbed a large, blanket-like towel and dropped it around Sally's shoulders. "You must be freezing. Let's go!"

Sally almost wished her friends had gotten as muddy as she had, so she could see if they would really shower in frigid water with their clothes on.

Wet, freezing, and wearing clothes that now weighed ten pounds more, Sally felt...disgruntled.

Kind of cranky, even.

She couldn't recall ever feeling cranky. *Ever.* She had always been pleasant. This new feeling was interesting, even though it was disagreeable.

As Essley propelled her down a tidy little street, Sally wondered how she could express this feeling. A facial expression? Some kind of characteristic walk? Insulting random passersby?

The first option had potential, but she dismissed the other two.

Aha! She knew! As Essley guided her up a set of wooden steps, Sally made a loud, snorting sound.

Essley froze. "What was that?"

"Disgust?" Sally answered hopefully.

Essley shook her head.

Sally looked to Darthrok for support.

"Nah," he said. "Sorry. That sounded more like 'heinous sinus infection' than 'disgust.' Try again."

Sally dug deep into her sense of dissatisfaction, thinking of her soggy feet inside her squishy boots. Her pretty boots.

Her pretty, *ruined* boots.

"Blehhhh!" she shouted.

A young adventurer who happened to be passing by leapt back, stumbled, and fell. Just as quickly, she rolled to her feet and hurried off in the direction she'd come.

Darthrok grinned at Sally. "Yeah, I think that'll do it. Good job!"

Sally laughed. He was half-teasing, but that was half the fun.

She was still giggling at her rude outburst as Essley

guided her into the haberdasher. Sally promptly forgot all about her amusement.

Who knew a fishing village had something like *this*?

"I should have come here sooner." Sally no longer felt the wet or the cold as she studied the racks upon racks of clothing and the outfits displayed on automatons which hung from the ceiling.

"Wow." She admired a small, but seemingly entirely functional hot air balloon mounted in the center of the store.

"I thought you might like it." Essley smiled, looking smug.

On cue, the store's CM swept into view. "Darling."

Sally did a double-take. She'd never seen a CM like this before.

He was the most glamorous, gorgeous thing she'd ever seen. Not handsome the way Sujan was, or beautiful like a woman either, but entirely his own kind of being.

And sparkly.

So sparkly.

His hair was longer than most men tended to wear, but he styled it almost straight up. Sally had never seen such facial symmetry, such full, pouty lips, or such defined eyebrows. Most strikingly, he had a tall, willowy frame, which he used to pose dramatically as he let them admire him.

Sally admired. She admired a lot.

"I'm James," he announced, as if he needed to. They could all see his name by looking at him. "And you…" he made a clicking sound with his tongue, "are downright tragic. What happened to you?"

"Scorpion," Sally answered. "Mud. Cold water."

She shivered.

"You poor darling." James swept toward her. "And those poor boots. What a loss! But this is what I'm here for, it's what I do. Let's make you shine."

He began propelling her toward a back room, as Essley had propelled her toward this store, but with more determination.

Sally looked behind her, toward her friends. "Is this good? Do I want to...shine?"

She was pretty sure she couldn't pull off a look with that much glitter and so many ruffles.

"Just link your account and do whatever he says," Essley advised. "I'm pretty sure this place was made for you. It's kind of like Raoul's, but all about you rather than where you live, and much more...well, *much*."

Sally threw a desperate look to Darthrok for confirmation, but he only shrugged and smiled.

James tugged her down a hallway that was dark, then bright red, then dark, then bright yellow, and continued changing every second. The strobing shift from dark to light made movements seem mechanical.

"Neat." She passed her hand in front of her face several times while James led her along. He paused, opened a door, and made a grand gesture like she'd won a major award and the prize was just inside.

"Hang on," she said. "Is there something terrible in there? Because this seems like a great way to kill someone."

He arched one immaculate eyebrow. "Do I look like someone who would dirty my store that way?"

"No. You really don't." She hoped he'd say more, but it seemed she'd received all the words from him that she'd get.

Sally nervously inched into the room. A light came on and Sally gasped. "How does it all fit?"

James smirked. "Magic, darling."

Sally stared up at what appeared to be eight stories of clothing display windows that encircled the room, which she realized was a dressing room.

He entered behind her and closed the door, standing next to a control panel of switches and levers.

"Let's get started," he declared. "Now, can I assume that this is your standard fashion?" He waggled his fingers at her wet clothes.

Embarrassed to be in such a haphazard state, Sally shrugged. "I like it."

"Are you willing to take some risks?" James grinned at her with a wolfish expression.

Why did this suddenly feel riskier than the scorpion confrontation? Sally longed to grab a socket wrench to hold, for its familiar weight and comfort.

"Some risk," she agreed slowly. "Not too much. I have to be a certain way. Not too...extreme."

"Hmm, a professional thing?" he asked, biting his lip thoughtfully and gazing up at the story upon story of displayed fashions.

She nodded. "Yes. Work."

"Gotcha. I'm going to ask you a series of questions, and I want you to answer with the first answer that comes to your mind, no thinking. Quick, quick like a bunny, got it?"

"Got it."

"Dresses or pants?" he demanded.

"Pants."

"Flowing or form-fitting?"

"Form-fitting." She carefully executed the tricky f-words with effort.

"Bright or muted?"

Sally hesitated. She liked both.

"Quick!" he snapped.

"Both!"

He smiled, but continued the interrogation. "What's one word that describes you?"

"Strong!"

"What's your favorite snack?"

"Churros!"

He put a hand to his chin, gazing at her intently. "Okay. One more. Do you have a boyfriend? Because I might need to marry you."

A laugh rose in Sally's throat, but James looked so serious she wasn't sure if he was joking. She didn't want to offend him if he'd fallen in love with her. "No."

"Is that no, you don't have a boyfriend, or no, you won't marry me?" His eyes sparkled with amusement.

Ah, he was teasing.

"Just no," Sally answered primly, then shot him a mischievous smile.

He laughed. "Fair enough. Okay, let's get started. Go behind the screen, please, and change into a robe. Those ruined clothes are making me sad."

She followed the direction of his pointing finger, then went to the other side of the thick, metal screen. Gratefully, she quickly peeled the sodden clothes from her skin, wiped off with a soft purple towel, and pulled on a silky pink dressing gown with a script pattern running down the long, flowing sleeves.

She felt fancy already.

Padding out in her bare feet, she smiled shyly at James.

"Hang on." He snapped his fingers. "There we go."

Sally put a hand to her hair, which had been hanging in wet tangles. It was now dry, styled, and glorious. "How did you—"

James cut her off. "Magic. I already told you. Try to keep up."

At Sally's bemused expression, he added, "It's unique to my shop. Nowhere else in Everternia does fashion come alive. Just go with it."

She didn't believe in magic. Not in the way he implied it, anyway. She suspected some deep-rooted mechanics, specific to James himself, but she decided to go with it. No one truly understood the world they lived in—herself included. Everyone just made their best guesses and assumptions and forged their way forward.

She'd do the same. "Okay."

He flashed her a brilliant smile. "Let's start with leather. I think you're a leather kind of girl."

Sally thought he was right.

James pulled a lever and the configuration of the towering stories of displays shifted. They expanded outward, allowing the fourth row up to slip between, slide down, and then compress together, with the other layers above, as they'd all started out.

"Wow."

"We're just getting started." James winked.

An hour later, Sally strode out to the main room of the store and struck a dramatic pose for her friends, just as James had instructed her.

"Whoa," Darthrok stood from the chair where he'd slumped during the long wait.

Essley turned from the display of elaborate hats she'd been examining. "Holy gasket."

Was that good? Sally hoped it was good.

The two of them came closer, gawking, and Sally still wasn't sure whether they were impressed or drawn in by some kind of can't-look-away-from-the-disaster energy.

Darthrok extended a finger to touch one of the many buckles that ran down Sally's bodice, but Essley slapped his hand away. "What the doot, dude!"

"What?" He froze.

"You can't just touch her!" Essley drew closer and touched the same buckle Darthrok had been eyeing.

"What, and you can?" Darthrok looked at Essley like she'd insulted his honor, and the honor of his family for three generations, retroactive in time.

"I'm her friend," Essley said, admiring the metalwork and leatherwork of Sally's new outfit. "This is amazing, Sally!"

"I'm her friend, too," Darthrok argued.

"You're a dude," Essley noted.

"I'm...she's..." Darthrok sputtered. "It's Sally. She's family. Sally doesn't think I'm a perv." He turned his attention to Sally. "Do you?"

Sally didn't know this word. She gathered that it meant something related to guys touching girls, and that it was violently frowned upon.

If frowns could be violent.

Sally kind of hoped they could.

She gave herself a mental shake. She was following too many trails of thought while her friends were looking at her for some kind of confirmation.

"Darthrok isn't a perv," she said carefully. "It's a neat outfit, and I'm family."

Darthrok smiled, vindicated.

Surprisingly, Essley smiled, too. "Okay then. I just didn't want him to make you uncomfortable."

Sally didn't understand why that might be the case, but she appreciated Essley's misplaced concern. Not long ago, no one at all felt any concern toward Sally, and she didn't plan to ever take that for granted. Even if Essley was being weird. Sally was weird, too, so it only made her feel closer to her friend.

"It's so sleek!" Essley said. "Isn't it uncomfortable?"

Sally tilted her shoulders and torso to the right, then the left, to show how the fabric moved with her. "It's great!"

"How much does something like that cost?" Darthrok asked.

"Twenty plat, since I bought so much other stuff. Bulk discount," Sally nodded, pleased with herself.

Essley's and Darthrok's jaws fell open at the exact same time as if choreographed.

Darthrok sounded choked. "How much did you spend, in all?"

"Two hundred plat even."

Their jaws somehow dropped further.

"What?" Sally asked, suddenly defensive.

"That's...a lot of coin," Essley said.

James burst into view, carrying two armfuls of bags. "You can't put a price on feeling your best. Which is what you get when you look your best. And doesn't she look un-steamin'-believable?"

James drew close and gestured at her with both hands as if revealing a great work of art.

Sally had to agree. She did feel great. And since money didn't mean anything to her, why shouldn't she buy whatever made her happy?

"Don't worry," James winked at Darthrok and Essley. "She has plenty more."

"She...does?" Essley looked from James to Sally.

Darthrok straightened. "Well...I guess you haven't had much to spend your money on before, right Sally? It would make sense that you have lots of money in your accounts. Right?"

Sally didn't have accounts like they did. They sometimes made the mistake of thinking she was like them, which she didn't mind because it was nice to be included. Being a CM, she could summon whatever money she wanted, at any time.

Given their reactions, she decided she'd been right in keeping her financial situation to herself.

"Right," she agreed. "I saved up."

"Well, you look amazing." Essley smiled.

"She looks more than amazing!" James exclaimed. "She's a vision. An inspiration. I'm going to create a whole line based on her. I'm going to call it..." He held his hands up in the air as if framing something, "Strongpunk Fashion. It's going to be huge."

"I'm sure it will," Darthrok agreed politely.

Essley simply nodded.

Sally sensed that her friends were overwhelmed by James' fabulousness, and she didn't blame them. He had about five levels of personality intensity, and seemed to be stuck on the highest level. He was just a *lot*.

She liked that about him.

"Huge!" James insisted.

Darthrok whispered in her ear, "I feel awkward when he talks. None of my answers could possibly be right."

Sally laughed. "Everybody's good," she assured him. "Just different."

James swept Sally into a big hug, kissed her on both cheeks, then pressed the bags into her hands. "You're doing great, sweetie. Just keep being you. And come see me soon. Strongpunk Fashion is going to be The Thing. And I'll owe it all to you."

Sally laughed. "I'll come again. Have good adventures."

James lifted his chin, looking heroic. Then he winked.

"Home?" Darthrok asked. "There's a bus coming in just a couple minutes."

"Oooh, bus," Sally agreed.

She'd do the whole ride standing up, this time. While holding her bags. Steaming gaskets, it was going to be so fun!

———

"NEED ANY HELP CARRYING THOSE?" Darthrok asked, gesturing at Sally's numerous shopping bags.

"Sure." She handed him a few of them. "Thanks."

"I'll take some, too," Essley offered.

Sally handed them off. If it were anyone else, she'd be worried about her new treasures, but she could trust Essley and Darthrok.

They arrived at the bus stop. When they'd arrived in Reel, the bus stop had been nothing but a spot on the road with a bench and a post that had a bus schedule attached. Upon their return, they found that an old woman had commandeered the bench and set a table in front of it.

Apparently, she was in business.

A glance told Sally that the CM had nothing she needed. She had no use for fishing poles and nets, or small water globes with aquatic scenes inside. The woman herself seemed interesting, though. Sally had never seen anyone so old. Her face had such deep wrinkles that they appeared to be ruts that had wrinkles of their own.

It was a nice face. A face with character. Sally assessed her.

Nan. CM.

Class: Entrepreneur.

Specialty: Streetmonger.

Nan's grandmotherly looks hide her nerves of steel. Unwary people underestimate her, and pay the price.

A streetmonger specialty? Sally hadn't seen anyone else associated with that word before.

"Ah, three young people waiting on a bus. You know what that makes?" Nan asked.

"What?" Darthrok asked.

Nan smiled slyly. "Time for you to buy something. Old ladies have to make a living too, you know."

"I'm sorry," Essley said. "But we aren't going fishing, and don't need souvenirs. But your goods look very nice."

"'Nice' doesn't buy Nan any dinner, now does it?"

Darthrok and Essley shifted uncomfortably.

"Do you have anything else?" Sally asked.

"Well, since you have time," Nan said coyly. "We could play a little game."

"What kind of game?"

A deck of cards materialized in Nan's hand. "So glad you asked. Here." She spread the cards and held them out, face-down, toward Sally. "Pick a card."

"I wouldn't," Darthrok said in a low voice.

"I would." Sally studied the backs of the cards, which all had the same levers and gears pattern on the back. She looked at Nan. Was Nan trying to encourage her to pick any particular card?

Didn't seem so. Sally selected one slightly right of center.

"Take a look, but don't show me," Nan instructed. "Memorize it. Better yet, show it to your friends."

Sally looked. Nine of spades. She showed the card to Essley and Darthrok, who both looked displeased to be going along with this.

"Put it back in, anywhere. I won't look." Nan turned her head, looking back over her shoulder, and held the deck out to Sally.

Sally slid the card back in among the others.

Nan shuffled the cards with an easy, practiced move. "Most people don't realize that their energy leaves a stamp on things. Once they've touched something, it's marked, like a piece of them. Not anything, mind you, only things of importance. And cards are particularly sensitive to that kind of energy."

"Really?" Sally watched Nan as she shuffled the cards again and again.

"Oh, yes. For example, watch. You've only touched one of these cards. I'll find it just by looking for your energy on it." Nan spread the cards out across the table, then bent closer, examining them closely.

"Ah, there it is." She plucked a card up and flicked it up for them to see. "That's the one."

Nine of spades.

"Yes, that's it," Sally agreed.

Nan turned it around, glanced at the card, then back at Sally, her expression guarded. "Right then. Now all you have to do is find your card. If I can do it, surely you can, right?"

Sally shook her head. "No, I don't do cards. I won't be good at it like you."

"What if we only use three cards?" Nan asked. She lay the nine of spades face-up on the table, and put two other cards on either side of it. "Just three, and you can watch my hands the whole time."

It seemed like a trick. Of course she could keep track of one card among only three. "Okay," Sally agreed.

Nan smiled. "Just keep your eye on the card. If you find

it, you get a prize. If you don't, you owe me a gold coin. But you'll find it, won't you?"

A trick. Nan had asked Sally to agree to the deal, which would bind her to it, and then she'd asked another question. Saying yes to either would obligate Sally to the deal, but in this case, she intended to agree anyway.

"Okay," she said again.

Nan began mixing the three cards, flipping them over the others, again and again. Her hands were a blur of motion, and sometimes almost entirely obscured the cards.

After a full minute of mixing them up, Nan took her hands away. "Which one is yours?"

Without hesitation, Sally pointed to the one on the left. "That one."

"You're sure?" Nan asked.

"Yes."

Nan flipped the card over to reveal the nine of spades. "Well done. You win a prize."

Darthrok patted Sally's shoulder. "Good job! I thought for sure it was the one in the middle."

"So did I," Essley added.

Nan had wanted her to choose the one in the middle. Sally had seen it in the way Nan moved the cards, and moved her hand into the way when she didn't need to. Nan was highly skilled at misdirection.

Nan gathered the cards. "I can't remember the last time someone won. Doesn't happen very often."

"I bet," Darthrok muttered, and Essley nudged him.

"What's the prize?" Essley asked.

Nan smiled. "The edge of a secret, the starting point of power. It's a special prize, one that no one's ever received. But it's only for the bold of heart. Do you want it? If you want the easy way, I can give you a platinum coin instead. Make your choice."

Darthrok and Essley both looked to Sally.

"It's a special quest," he said. "A one-time thing that no one else has ever done. Do you want to?"

Sally didn't even have to take the time to ponder. "Special quest. I want the special quest."

Nan smiled. "I had a feeling about you. Not anyone could do this, but maybe you can. I've been waiting for someone special."

Nan pulled something from her pocket and held her closed fist out, waiting.

Sally put her palm under the fist.

Nan opened her hand, and Sally felt something drop into her palm. Looking at it, she saw a cotter pin.

No, it wasn't just a cotter pin. Looking closer, Sally saw that the pin was also a key. It had a tiny pattern on its bottom side, which surely was designed to unite with an opposing pattern to unlock...what?

Her curiosity bloomed, creating a thrill of excitement. "What is it?"

"In a place protected by legs, you'll find shadows and dust. If you look beyond the gloom, you'll find the heart. *This* will make the heart beat again." Nan smiled mysteriously.

Sally pinched the cotter pin key between her thumb and forefinger.

"Great wealth can come from it, or great misfortune. Choose wisely."

"Sounds kinda bad," Darthrok whispered. "Think we can trade it in for the platinum coin?"

Sally shot him a look of disgust. Where was his sense of adventure? She hadn't woken up to play it safe and avoid excitement. And Jin had told her to "give them a steamin' heck of a time." Surely this was an opportunity to do that.

She closed her fist around the cotter pin key. She caught Nan's gaze, looked deep, and said, "What would you do?"

Nan's gaze flickered, looking into Sally's eyes. For a moment, Sally almost saw something...something almost like awareness. "I'd go all in, child. No risk, no reward."

Sally nodded. "I'll do it. All the risk. All the reward. And I'll come tell you about it after."

Nan's gaze sharpened even further. "You do that, child. You do that."

Behind them, the bus slid into view with a dramatic *swoosh* of released steam and the musical sound of gears swapping out to reduce speed to a stop.

What a wonderful, soothing sound.

The old woman's eyes lost their focus, went vague, then roamed over Sally's shoulder. "Ah, a young man waiting on a bus. You know what that makes?" Nan asked.

Sally turned to follow her gaze, seeing a young cook behind her. She could tell at a glance that he had no coin to spend.

How sad. If she hadn't had a gold coin to risk, she'd never have gotten the treasure she held within her fist.

With a pointed look at her friends, Sally said, "Stay well, Nan. I'll visit again."

Nan paid her no mind, but as Sally passed the cook to board the bus, she pressed a gold coin into his palm. She wouldn't miss it, and it might just lead to the biggest adventure of his life.

Smiling, Sally stood in the center of the bus, grabbed a strap, and prepared for a glorious ride back to Pivot.

11

SALLY RETURNED TO HER STORE, bags in hand, feeling like a billion platinum.

No, more than that. Way more. She'd always had all the coins she needed. Now, she had things that were worth far more. Things that couldn't be bought with money.

Essley and Darthrok had gone to see to some of their own personal business, so she was alone when she unlocked her store.

Hang on.

That was fun.

She locked the door again, then unlocked it a second time, just because she could.

So cool!

Having a lock for the door was fantastic!

Once she got into the store, though, she felt a wave of dissatisfaction. Yes, her seating area was inviting and she looked forward to sitting there soon. Her cash register stood ready as ever for when customers arrived.

But she had numerous new garments and accessories, and nowhere appropriate to put them.

She wasn't about to store them in the cabinets that held her wares for sale. No way. But where then?

She didn't want to keep her personal things in the main part of her store. That only left the control room, which had no storage other than a maintenance box for the navigation and propulsion systems.

Unhappy with her options but with nothing she could do about it for the moment, she left her bags in the control room. At least James would have packed her treasures away carefully to prevent wrinkles. She felt certain of that.

Thinking of him made her smile. She hoped she could see him again soon. Instinct told her that Pivot would be shifting soon, though, so it could be a while, especially if they ended up far away from Reel.

In the meantime, she had a quest to complete.

Essley and Darthrok had chatted a bit about what the quest might mean, but Sally had pretended not to overhear. She'd wanted to enjoy the bus ride and the lurching around without distraction.

Plus, she was pretty sure she already knew what the quest meant. More or less.

Unzipping a small hip pocket in her new pants—she loved these pants—she extracted the cotter pin key.

Pausing next to her cash register, which had once been enough for her, she realized she needed not only living quarters but a workspace. Because she had some serious work to do.

On the other hand...if this quest went the way she thought it would, she'd soon have more workspace than she currently knew what to do with.

Maybe Sujan would have some opinions. When the time came.

She continued to the control room of her store, where

she'd been keeping all of her personal things. From a tall, black-and-white striped hatbox, she retrieved a fist-sized device.

In spite of frowning over it often, trying to apply all of her newly-won knowledge of engineering and technie craft, she hadn't discerned its purpose.

But Nan had given her the key. Literally.

Sally shifted the device, exposing the bottom, which had a tiny hole. She'd thought it must be some sort of reset activation, but now she knew better.

She inserted the cotter pin key, sliding it effortlessly into place.

Then she waited, her right hand cradling the device.

It warmed in her palm, and she felt a motor start cycling. Its rhythm hummed against her skin, satisfyingly regular.

The frequency of the motor increased until it emitted a steady hum, sounding wonderfully alive. A yellow light lit.

Then it cycled down. The hum slowed to an occasional whir. The light remained on.

Sally waited, but that was it.

Nan had called it, "*The edge of a secret, the starting point of power.*"

Sally knew where she needed to go next.

IT WASN'T a convenient time for a shift, but Sally didn't have any influence over such matters. When Pivot shifted, everyone had to comply. Unfortunately, this move was going to be particularly inconvenient for her.

A bit boring, too. Darthrok had gone off on a hunting expedition, and he expected to be gone for a couple of days. Essley also needed to go abroad, in search of some medicinal plants. That left Sally without her friends, unable to solve the puzzle of the factory, and without an apprentice to help out with the store.

She studied with Sujan most days, but lately he only tolerated her for a couple hours each day. That was okay since she'd gotten to the point where she could grasp more complex tasks and could only do so much learning per day. She'd tried forcing more new knowledge into her brain, but it just didn't stick. Knowing her limits, she now worked within them more effectively.

It left her a little bored, though.

She still liked helping customers, but she needed more than that. A lot more.

As she leaned against the counter, waiting for another customer to arrive, she thought about what she could do to fill the time.

She left the sales room and went to the control center. She'd been putting her personal possessions in there, stacking them in the corner or hanging them from hooks on the wall. Maybe she could do something with this space. She only needed a small amount of room to access the store's navigation systems. Half of the cockpit could easily be converted into some personal quarters.

Too bad James couldn't do it. He'd make something amazing, for sure. Raoul's Nice Digs store ought to have great things. She just wouldn't have James' flair in putting them together. No matter. She'd do it in her own, particular style.

She'd need a wardrobe with doors, she decided, and some shelves. Maybe a dressing table. She didn't need a bed, since she rarely slept, but maybe a piece of convertible furniture that could be a place to sit or lie down.

Hm. Yes. It would work. She'd make this space her own.

Returning to the sales room, she waited for a customer to arrive. Slow day. Well, she didn't have to be bored. She'd take matters into her own hands and do something constructive.

Locking the door behind her, she set out to do some shopping.

"I'M UNIMPRESSED WITH THIS SHIFT," Sally said to no one at all. As with most shifts, business was slow after Pivot moved to a new location. In this case, it had moved particularly far, and as far as Sally could tell, there was nothing at all within many, many miles.

She was in the middle of nowhere, but that wasn't the problem. Her unhappiness came from being more than two hundred miles further away from the factory.

"Un. Im. Pressed," she repeated, enunciating each syllable like a legit pro talking-type-person. She looked upward and shook her fist at whatever powers controlled Pivot's shifts.

Actually...it was nice, being able to express her dissatisfaction. Before she woke up, she'd never done that. So she shook her fist again and tried her darnedest to come up with a good curse upon the powers-that-be.

"What the plonk, you doot-doot smidges."

She quite liked that, actually. It made her feel better. She committed the phrase to memory, for future reference.

She felt better already. So what if she was hundreds of miles from her destination, and her friends were busy with other things, and her mentor was a crusty fussbucket? She had herself, and that was all she needed.

The fact that things hadn't worked out as she'd planned

was just an opportunity for an adventure she'd never imagined.

Awesome!

Hmm. What to put in her backpack? Would she need a change of clothes? It didn't seem an unreasonable thing to plan for, so she carefully rolled up an outfit into a tidy burrito and tucked it into her pack.

Oh, man. She suddenly felt hungry for a burrito. She'd tried one recently, and had become an instant fan. Maybe she'd have the chance to try more new foods on this trip.

What else should she pack? She didn't need much to keep her comfortable. A brush for her hair, probably. Money. She grasped her *Mechanical Theory* book and tucked it into the back of the pack, then added *Supply Chain Management Essentials* in case she got bored of Mechanical Theory. Should she pack *Practical Electricity* too?

Nah. That would make her pack heavier than it needed to be. She'd stick with just the two books to fill her travel time.

Looking around at her meager belongings, she saw nothing else that seemed necessary. Just for her comfort, she packed a variety of basic tools, taking care to avoid anything too heavy.

With a shrug and a sigh, she picked up the pack and went out to the store room. There, she emptied the cash register into her pack.

There. She was as prepared as she could be for her first solo adventure. She slid her arms through the straps and settled her pack comfortably on her back.

She hesitated. Was she ready for this? To handle the world without Darthrok and Essley along to translate for her if she got confused about how things worked?

And could she leave the store for a day or more, until

Essley could get to it? She'd never been away from it for so long. What if customers got upset or were inconvenienced?

Sally let out a slow breath and straightened her spine. She could do this. Essley and Darthrok were dear to her, but she no longer needed to rely on them to follow her heart and find her own adventures.

She was all she needed. There was nothing that Everternia could spring on her that she couldn't handle.

She was enough. She'd never realized that before, but now she felt confident in herself and her ability to deal with things as they came along.

Resolutely, she strode out of her store and locked the door behind her.

TRAIN STATIONS WERE *AMAZING*.

Why hadn't she done this before? There was an intersection of activity and motion and information that became one big blur of buzzing possibility.

Sally had never seen a place with so many people or so much activity.

This was adventure! Excitement! There was even some random trash on the floor!

What a place!

She doubted her fellow travelers appreciated the wonder of it all even half as much as she did.

Poor people.

Sally followed the flow of traffic leading into the grand building, then slowed her pace to give herself a chance to figure out what to do next. She saw signs with labels like "Departures" and "Arrivals" and "Tickets," which all seemed wonderfully self-explanatory.

She appreciated logical transparency. It sure made life a lot easier.

With a casual but steady stride, she made her way toward the ticket booth. She'd have walked faster, but there was so much to take in and she didn't want to miss anything.

A sweeping, buttressed ceiling rose high overhead, and it was decorated in light-reactive paint. A scene of wildlife flowed into a night sky, which flowed into a painting of some dude with a big, frizzy mustache and beard. The large paintings, which curved along with the dimension of the ceiling, were interesting enough, but light rigs mounted to the ceiling shifted at regular intervals, creating different versions of the same painting.

Under red light, the wildlife scene became one of flames and smoke. Under purple light, the sky image turned into an aurora borealis. When blue light shined on the bearded guy, he somehow lost all the brushy facial hair and suddenly looked very handsome.

So cool.

When she arrived at the ticket window, Sally was ready. She'd practiced the words ahead of time to be sure she'd be able to say them properly.

The moment of truth arrived. "One round-trip ticket to Bracket, please."

Nailed it!

"Coach, upgraded, or a private room?" The automaton gazed at her blankly.

She hadn't prepared for this question. She looked around, making sure no one was close enough to overhear, and leaned in to ask in a low voice, "What's the difference?"

"About fifty gold, from one upgrade to the next."

That wasn't what she'd meant. She'd have to just choose something. A private room sounded uninteresting because she probably wouldn't be able to see much. So did she want coach or upgraded?

Coach was probably what most people chose, and since she was riding the train for the first time, she might as well start at the beginning. She mentally practiced the word a few times before carefully saying, "Coach, please."

"Ten gold."

Sally handed the coins over and received a key card in exchange. She waited to see if she needed to do anything else to finalize the transaction.

"Did you need something else?" the automaton asked.

"Um, no. Thank you." She hurried away.

Platform G. Sally paused to examine a map of the train station, which illustrated the layout of the various areas. Very logical. Nice.

Since she only had five minutes to board, Sally hurried on to Platform G, not taking the time to notice all the other people hurrying by her. She kept a firm hold on her objective so she didn't get distracted by all the adventurers and CMs streaming by.

Normally, she might get *very* distracted by all that.

Sally was still easily distractible, she found as she hurried along without leaping from foot to foot so that she could reasonably claim that she wasn't running, but *walking*, in compliance with the posted, stern warnings.

Totally following the rules. Yep.

As she rounded a corner that revealed the platform itself, Sally saw something irresistible. Never mind the excitement of the terminal itself, and all the implications of goings and arrivings, and all the adventures that implied. That was great, but...

Churros. And candy floss. And something called samosas.

Sally couldn't resist the siren call of sugar, and found herself drifting toward the tiny stand and its incredible aromas like a helpless little moth drawn toward a bright, shining flame.

The smell! Like cinnamon and sugar and angelic fruits had done a dance of joy that resulted it universal harmony. Surely no one could resist such a thing.

Before she knew up from down, Sally had purchased enough candy floss and churros to fortify a small village. She also bought some of the cute, fat little triangles called samosas. They didn't smell sweet, but had a wonderful aroma of their own.

At least, it seemed that way to her when she boarded the train with her hands full, bags of candy floss tucked into her armpits, and everything else clutched to her chest.

Had she made a mistake? Had she gone too far?

No way!

Sally found her seat easily since the seating system was as logical as the station's layout had been.

Upon wedging her behind into its assigned narrow perch, she immediately sensed that things had gone awry.

She might have chosen wrong when she selected "coach." It had sounded so nice. Like there'd be someone to cheer her on. But this...no. This felt more like a size-eight foot being shoved into a size-seven shoe.

And Sally was the foot.

"Dude," said the thug seated across from her, disconcertingly facing her and making more eye contact than she felt comfortable with. He was far larger than she, but he somehow seemed at ease in his too-small seat. He gestured to her extreme burden of candy floss and churros. "Them's some *snacks.*"

He gave her a thumbs-up, and she decided that her

initial impression might have been wrong. She might not have to pound him into the dirt at some point in the near future.

Maybe this steam train ride could still be cool, if she tried. Surely there was some fun in it somewhere, if she looked hard enough.

"Last call for west world line, stops at Grommet, Hinge, Lazy Susan, and Bracket. Last call!"

Sally waited, clutching her snacks awkwardly and trying not to pay too much attention to the eager thug across from her, just because he seemed like he *wanted* to get her attention.

After a couple of minutes, Sally felt, rather than heard, the swell of applied steam energy.

"Doors secured. Commencing forthwith!"

Forthwith? Who said that? Sally looked around, but saw no one who appeared to be the speaker.

Thug Dude across from her tilted his head to the side, glancing at the seat next to her. "Bet you can put your snacks there. Empty seat. Relax."

Cautiously, Sally looked around then carefully piled her paper-wrapped churros and bundles of candy floss into the unoccupied seat next to her.

Except for one bunch of pink and blue candy floss, because yum. She kept it in her lap alongside the paper-board box of samosas.

She set her backpack in the next seat, too, for the moment. If someone came to sit in that seat, she'd put it in the overhead bin, but she didn't want to do that until she was sure she had whatever she needed from it. She just wasn't sure yet what she'd need.

She pulled off a piece of the sweet candy fluff and pushed it into her mouth, letting the sugar melt away to nothing on her tongue. Structurally speaking, candy floss was kind of a miracle. It seemed to occupy multiple states of matter simultaneously.

Thug Dude sat, watching her.

A couple of soft bumps and a minor sense of accelera-tion indicated that the journey had begun. She paused, waiting for something interesting to happen. Trains went much faster than buses, so she hoped to be able to feel the movement even more. So far, though...nothing.

She leaned out into the aisle, looking for straps for standing passengers to hold, but there were none. There were no standing passengers, either, actually.

"What are you looking for?" Thug Dude asked.

"Straps," she said.

"What, like on the bus? Nah, not here. It's a good hour before we get to the first stop, and most people are going further than that. Everyone gets a seat on the train, even though they're small back here in coach. Guessing this is your first trip?"

She didn't like admitting that she was so unworldly, but she nodded.

"The good news," he said, "is that it's not going to feel like much. You'll just be sitting here. But the bad news is that, well, you'll just be sitting here. It gets boring fast. If you're on one of the later stops, it's a lot of empty time to fill."

Bracket was the last stop. After all the delays at other stations, it would take about four hours to get to Bracket.

Four very *boring* hours, apparently.

She should have bought more snacks.

The thug was watching her curiously and she realized she hadn't said anything, which was a bit rude. She picked up a paper-wrapped order of churros and held it out to him. Then she opened the box of samosas and held it out to him.

"Let's do our best," she said.

He took the treat and smiled, his previously insolent expression transforming him. He became good-looking, with a light of warmth in his eyes. She also saw a hint of mischief.

"I'm Sally," she added.

"Rex," he said. He took a big bite of cinnamon-coated dough and chewed. He gave her a nod of thanks. With his other hand, he took a samosa.

Sally bit into one of the puffy triangles and blew out a quick breath to cool the hot filling. How could it still be so hot? But it was. It was steaming. After a few huffed breaths, she chewed the samosa. *Mmm. Yummy!* Definitely different than anything she'd tried so far.

The ate their treats in silence, and Sally wondered how she'd fill so much time. Most travelers probably slept, but that wouldn't work for her. Pulling *Practical Electricity* from her backpack, she set it on her lap and reached for some churros.

"Whoa." Rex leaned forward to get a better look at the book. "That looks like some heavy reading."

Sally bounced her knees, making the book move up and down. "Not really. Paper doesn't weigh much."

He laughed and sat back, getting comfortable in his seat. "You're funny. I like that. You don't meet too many funny technies."

"You don't?" This was news to her.

"Nah. They tend to be super serious. No offense."

She shrugged. "Thugs aren't that funny, either, most of the time."

He grinned. "Fair enough."

A silence fell, and Sally felt awkward, so she picked up a bag of candy floss and held it out to him.

"You sure? You weren't saving this for someone?"

"No," she answered. "It's just good. I bought lots."

"Well, all right, then. Thanks." He accepted the bag and opened it. "I'll return the favor sometime."

Was that an actual promise, or was it just something that people said? Not knowing for sure, Sally just nodded and turned her attention to her book.

"What stop are you going to?" he asked.

"Bracket."

"End of the line. Long trip. I'm going to Lazy Susan, so I'll be getting off at the stop right before yours."

Why was he telling her this? Was he just making conversation? Did he expect her to remark on his destination? How should she handle his friendliness? She hadn't been prepared for it.

But she supposed she'd started it by giving him the churros.

She'd try her best. Given her history with adventurers and how often they'd treated her badly in the past, she had reservations about trusting any of them. Other than Essley and Darthrok, of course. Rex was a thug and had a rough edge to him, but that didn't mean he couldn't be a friend, at least for a few hours.

What trouble could happen on board a train, anyway?

Rex arched an eyebrow and smiled at her. It was a particular kind of smile that gave her a feeling that a lot of trouble could be found anywhere, if the right person came along.

"Ever think about robbing a train?" she asked.

His smile grew. "What did you have in mind? Whatever it is, I'm in."

Sally laughed. "Just asking."

He nodded, still smiling. "All right, fair enough. But if you think of something, let me know."

"You like adventure?"

"Sure, what else is there? Isn't that why we're all here? Even you techies and the scholar types, everyone's looking for the kind of adventure they find fun, right?"

Sally turned her book sideways on her lap and rested her hands on it. "Everyone's looking for something here."

"Exactly," he said a little too loudly, causing a few people to glance over. He paid them no mind. "It's like, if Reallife had everything we wanted already, we wouldn't be spending our time here. So we're looking for what can only be found in this place."

He was from Reallife, like Essley and Darthrok? What a coincidence. She wondered if they knew him.

"I've never been to Reallife," she admitted. "I've been too busy so far."

He laughed, showing two rows of big, even teeth. "Hard-core role player, huh? That's cool. I try to stay in character, but then I start running my mouth and my brain doesn't always keep up."

He must be saying things that only other thugs would understand. She smiled politely. She hadn't spent much time with adventurers, and so far, he believed that she was a regular adventurer like him. She didn't want to mess that up.

"So what are you going to do in Bracket?" he asked. "Are there some parts you have to buy for making stuff?"

"Something like that," she agreed. "What about you?"

"I've got some stuff stored in a locker in Lazy Susan, and a buddy wants to buy it. I'll probably hunt while I'm there, too, because why not?"

"Got to keep the learning going," she said.

"Exactly. Do you get ranks for reading books like that?" He eyed the one in her lap.

"A little. It used to be more but it's harder to advance now."

He made a sound that was remarkably like that of a large steam engine. "It's like that, isn't it? Grind, grind, grind. Isn't much different than Reallife, is it?" He grimaced. "Sorry. There I go again. Ignore that. What I mean is, if it's all just work anyway, why bother? I've been thinking of taking a break from all this. That's why I'm selling off some of my stuff. I mean, if it isn't fun anymore, what's the point, right?"

Reallife sounded like a bummer. No wonder people left it. Maybe she didn't want to visit it, after all. He sounded like he wanted her to agree with him about the futility of his life, but she couldn't.

"Maybe don't grind, if you don't like it," she said.

"What do you mean?"

"If it's not fun and you don't like it, then do something else. Find your own type of fun."

His lips pressed together, and his big personality seemed to dial itself down as he grew serious. "What do you find fun, Sally Strong?"

It was a good question.

"I like new things. I like friends. I like laughing and growing. Those are the best."

"So maybe if I stop working my ranks all the time and ease off the leveling, I could...what? What would I do?"

"You have friends?" she asked.

"Yeah. I mean, they'd gut me to steal from me if they could, but we hang out."

"Sounds like not good friends," she observed. "My friends make me happy."

"Well," he said, "I do tend to hang out with ratfinks and schmucks."

Sally brightened. These were new words. She resolved to try them out in the near future in regard to people who were up to no good. "Find new friends. You'll be happier."

"Maybe you're right." He looked at her, apparently in deep contemplation. "Maybe I'm hanging with the wrong crowd. But, let's be real. Look at me. You think people like that would make friends with a guy like me? I'm a thug."

Sally shrugged. She saw nothing wrong with him. So he was big and brawny. There was nothing wrong with him. He looked like a thug, sure, but he also had tons of Easterner charisma. Everything about him was big and bright and filled the room, from his laugh to his big smile to how very thoughtful he looked when he got serious. "You're as worthy as anyone else."

"Am I?" he leaned forward, his gaze intent on her. He extended his left hand slowly, toward the book on her lap. He put a finger on the corner of the book. "Are you saying you're not afraid of me right now?"

She returned his gaze, unflinching. "No. You don't scare me."

"Why not? I should."

"You like churros, like I do. You have a nice smile. You're looking for something, like me. I'm looking, too. Everyone's looking. Why would you scare me?"

"Have you assessed me?" he asked.

She assessed him.

Rex

Adventurer

Unlawful Neutral

Level Sixty-two

Profession: Entrepreneur

Specialty: Thug

Rex is carrying six platinum coins.

Rex has nine hundred and twenty-eight platinum, sixty-seven gold, forty-eight silver, and two copper in electronic funds.

Rex is a formidable adversary, but not a concern for you.

Rex's karma is bad.

Rex reminds you of a lost puppy.

She smiled. "Have *you* assessed *me*?"

"What?"

She kept smiling, and he narrowed his eyes, looking at her with increased intensity.

"Hang on," he said. "You could pound me into the dirt? What? How? You gonna beat me with your screwdriver?"

Sally grinned. "If I have to. But I'm better at taking things apart, piece by piece, from their foundation."

Holy gasket, that sounded so cool! She'd gotten every word out just right, without slipping on any of the vowels.

For the first time since she met him, Rex looked uncertain. "Who are you?"

"Not sure yet," she admitted. "I'm figuring it out."

"Maybe I should stick around a little bit," he mused. "Are you married, Sally?"

"To my screwdriver. Don't get ideas."

He laughed. "Fair enough, fair enough. Okay. So, how do you feel about having some company in Bracket?"

She looked at him curiously.

"Nothing weird," he showed his palms. "Friend-zone is fine with me, so long as we both know it. I just..." he hesitated, again showing an uncertainty that she sensed was unusual for him. "This is the most fun I've had for as long as

I can remember, and we haven't done anything but eat snacks and talk."

He shrugged helplessly.

"Okay," she said. "Come with me. You can help."

"Help with what? I don't know anything about...you know, electricity or that kind of stuff." He looked embarrassed. "All I do is smash things."

She smiled. "Sometimes, a smash works best."

"HANG ON," Rex said.

Sally paused, adjusting her backpack so it settled more comfortably on her back. "Yes?"

"There's a clicker swarm at that old wreck. The higher your rank, the more they spawn." Rex frowned at the factory in the distance. "Nobody goes *inside*. Well, at least, they don't go there *twice*."

"Why?"

"It's a trap!" he said. "No matter how good you are, the clickers will engage you, keep you from leaving, then swarm and kill you, one hit point at a time. It's a known kill point. The more people you bring, the more clickers that spawn. And there's no reason to even go in there. That factory's worthless. Nothing at all valuable inside. You just die for no reason."

His ignorance made her sad.

"What's inside is all pieces," she explained. "Pieces that aren't valuable alone. But together..." She snapped her fingers. "Together, it's treasure."

"What do you mean?" he asked. "How's that disaster zone a treasure?"

Even if Sally had the words to explain it to him, she

wouldn't. The factory was too important to her. The fact that she'd even brought him seemed crazy, but she felt like this challenge would matter to him. He'd implied that he wasn't having any fun anymore, which was sad.

His help would also improve her chances of success.

"It's a puzzle," she explained. "A quest. It's meant to be solved."

He sighed. "I never heard about any quest here. Just a bunch of slow, stupid death."

She smiled at him. "First time solve. You'll get lots of experience."

He narrowed his eyes, and a hint of smile appeared. "Don't you sweet talk me, now."

"*So* much experience," she reiterated. "And you can have it all. I just want the factory."

"Who are you?"

She stiffened. "What?"

"You're like, super wise sometimes, but the way you talk is kind of unusual sometimes. And now you're a technie kamikaze or something. I don't know what to do with all that."

She squinted at him. "*What?*"

"Nothing." His shoulders slumped, then he straightened. "Fine. Whatever. I've died for dumber reasons. Let's do it."

She held up her fist and stretched it toward him. "Yeah!"

Shaking his head, he gave her a fist-bump.

"What do I do?" he asked.

"Tank it up." She pointed at the front entrance to the factory. "Go there, get aggro. Keep doing that."

"And what will you be doing?"

She shrugged off one strap of her backpack to slide it sideways and reach into it. She pulled out the device she'd taken, plus the cotter pin, and inserted it. It lit up from within. She held it out for him and said, "Storming the castle."

She'd heard Darthrok say the phrase once, and she'd liked it, and practiced it, just in case she ever had a chance to use it.

Woohoo! Objective achieved. She put the device back and re-secured her pack.

His face showed surprise. "Oh, hey, you're about to go full mad scientist, aren't you? Dang, I didn't know you guys did that."

"Maybe we don't usually," she said, "but I'm going to."

"All right, Sally girl, let's see what happens." He pulled a long, massively-heavy looking sword from its sheath.

He waded in, and as soon as he reached the entrance, a flood of clickers rushed out, stopping him from entering. He began chipping away at the little mechies, and Sally ran to the back side of the factory. She scanned the outside, then her eye caught on what she needed.

There! A service ladder. All those skylight windows had needed to be cleaned at some point, or even replaced if one cracked. From her backpack, she retrieved a long, tele-scoping reaching pole with a hook at the end. James had used them in his store to reach merchandise that was displayed high, and Sally had thought the tool might come in handy someday.

Today was that day!

She extended the pole to its full length, glanced around for clickers, then reached for the ladder.

Miss! The pole swished by the ladder, hit the side of the building, and began a fast slide down to the ground. She hadn't planned for how unwieldy the pole would be at full length. She tried again. Miss.

On the third try, she hooked the ladder and pulled it down. Yes!

After collapsing the reaching hook and returning it to her backpack, she climbed.

No clickers so far, which was good.

Stepping up onto the roof, she looked around again. Anything?

No. Her theory that clickers could only walk on the ground was holding up, so far. As long as she didn't step on the ground, she shouldn't get mobbed by them.

She hoped.

She also hoped Rex was doing okay, but she didn't want to use the communicator and risk distracting him.

Okay, there had to be a way into the factory from the roof. An access hatch, something. She hurried along, looking for easy access. If she needed to, she could break a window in the skylight, but that would be a shame and difficult to replace.

Just when the window-breaking method was looking more and more likely, she saw an air intake vent.

Yes!

With the screwdriver Rex had made fun of, she quickly opened the vent and peered inside.

"Yuck!"

Darkness and many layers of dust. Well, she'd prepared for that, too, by changing into her current, entirely fashion-free outfit. The long-sleeved top and long pants had no zippers or catches, and looked like something that people should only ever sleep in, if that.

But it would work well for this task and keep her good clothes from getting ruined.

Sally flipped her goggles down and settled them over her

eyes, then flipped to the illumination lenses. They were a poor substitute for a torchlight because they didn't project straight ahead, but she'd decided to use them to keep her hands free. This would be good enough to get her through some ductwork.

Twenty minutes later, coughing and brushing her hand over her goggles to clear them of dust, a bit of doubt crept in. But after another five minutes of belly-crawling and regretting her decisions, she regretted them even more when a steep decline sent her sliding on her belly to who-knows-where.

Some things only seemed like a good idea before actually doing them.

Then she found another grate.

She removed this one even faster than the first, then poked her head out. She was inside the factory, but about halfway up the wall, which put her a good twenty feet from the ground.

That was okay. She had no intention of touching the ground. Yet. She had small goals to accomplish before she could achieve the main objective.

One thing at a time.

She hoped Rex was okay. Getting him killed on the day they met probably wasn't a good way to start a friendship.

After pulling a large, folded square of fabric from her pack, she carefully unrolled a brief length of it, tied it around a sturdy pipe, and pushed the rest of the fabric out into the factory. It fell, unfolding as it went, until it hung in a long, straight line.

She hadn't been confident in her ability to slide down a rope. But she'd studied the mechanics of aerial silks, and was confident that she could manage to make her way down one of them. She'd practiced the foot locks in her store, and was pretty sure she could do this.

Turning around to lie on her belly, she edged backward, dangling her feet out of the opening, then continued until she could bend at the waist. This was the tricky bit. Blindly, she reached for the silk with her feet, found it, and wrapped it around her foot so that she'd have a solid hold.

She took a breath. Moment of truth.

Grasping the top of the cloth, she shifted her weight to her silk-wrapped foot.

She now dangled twenty feet above the factory, suspended in cloth by one foot. She couldn't wait to tell Darthrok and Essley about this.

While bending at the knee, she used her other foot to reach down and flip the fabric around her ankle, her heel, then across her forefoot, which gave her a solid lock. She shifted her weight to that foot. Nice! Now, about fifteen more times, and she'd be done.

Her arms ached with the unexpected stress, even though her legs were doing most of the work. She tried to ignore the discomfort as she descended foot by foot. By the time she made the last motion, her arms were shaking, but she didn't want to drop down because she wasn't sure how strong the worktable below was. She could just imagine crashing down on it, having it break, falling to the floor, and getting swarmed by clickers.

Better to avoid that.

At last, she got one foot on the table, and kicked the fabric off her second foot so she could stand solidly on two feet.

Her arms hated her. A lot.

But she'd done it! She'd made it into the factory, and by not touching the floor, she hadn't inadvertently summoned any mechies.

She looked up at the long swathe of fabric dangling

down into the factory. It would be tricky getting that back down, but she'd think about that later.

From her current spot, she needed to make three good leaps to get to her destination. A loud noise outside caught her attention. Rex? She should probably hurry.

Given the leg placement of these tables and their weight distribution, she could only go halfway beyond the center to the farther edge to gain momentum. If she moved further back, the table would likely fall over.

Okay. One big step, then a leap to the next table. She could do this.

Careful not to step too far to either side of the table, she stepped back, then launched herself forward.

Too close to the edge! She stumbled forward, trying to direct the bulk of her weight toward the center of the table. It tipped slightly, but settled with her kneeling in the center, her heart pounding.

Success! She just had to do the same thing two more times.

The next jump went a little better than the first.

The final jump started out well, then quickly went wrong. Somehow, she landed too far forward, putting her too far away from the center of the table. She fell forward, onto her knees, catching herself on the edge and pushing back quickly.

Don't fall, don't fall, don't fall.

The table tipped, and the surface beneath her slammed to the floor, tossing her off. She sprawled across the dirty floor.

Scrambling to her feet, she raced to the machine at the center of the factory. She jumped up on it—not because it would keep the clickers from coming, because she could hear them already. But if she was lucky, they might not be able to reach her if she stayed off the floor.

She could still do this. She just needed to be quicker and smarter than the mechies.

Nan had said, "*In a place protected by legs, you'll find shadows and dust. If you look beyond the gloom, you'll find the heart. This will make the heart beat again.*"

She knew exactly what she needed to do.

Carefully, she made her way to the center of the machine, which wasn't easy, because it wasn't meant to be walked on. She had to find handholds and toegrips that had never been designed as such. But she got there.

She took off her backpack and put it down, opening it to pull out the device she'd taken from here on a day that felt so long ago.

She inserted the cotter pin key and the device—the heart—lit. Carefully positioning her feet, she braced her thighs against the machine and leaned her body into the very center of the it.

Holding her breath, she slid the gadget into the wide-open slot she remembered from her first visit here. She gave the heart a firm push.

It clicked into place.

The sound of the clickers grew loud, and she looked over her shoulder to see them swarming in, nearly obscuring the entire floor.

She hoped Rex was okay.

She felt a heaving churn that restarted the machine, kicking it into gear, and it whirred to life. The sound it made grew louder and higher until it generated enough energy to throw the lights on and bring the other machines alive. The factory hummed with unending possibility.

Still standing at the center of it all, she wrapped her

arms around the long pipe, feeling it coming alive and shivering with energy.

She knew how it felt. She felt the same. A feeling of power filled her. This factory belonged to her now.

The heart was beating.

The clickers paused. She looked to them. "Go hibernate."

Immediately, they shuffled off, disappearing through small cracks and openings, returning to their place in the subbasement to wait for her call.

When the cascade of tiny mechies ended, and the last had disappeared, Rex staggered in, looking rough but in no immediate danger.

He saw her, in the center of it all, and stared. "What did you do?"

She smiled. "I pushed the right button. That's all."

He grinned. "I think you're lying. But it's cool."

She laughed and walked toward him. The experience bonus hit him and he froze, then began shouting in celebration. Whatever he'd gotten must have been wonderfully good.

"You shouldn't have let me have it all," he said after a wild victory dance. "Not that I'm sad about it."

She didn't care about the experience. She had the factory and all its future wonders. Nothing could compare to that.

It was hers, this place. She'd do something wonderful with it. Having a store and helping people was nice, but the endless possibilities in front of her made her heart soar and opened up her mind to new possibilities.

This wasn't what others thought she was. This was what she *really* was.

She was alive and ready for what came next.

12

———

"It's incredible, Sal. Really." Darthrok stood in the center of her factory, taking it all in.

"But?" Sally knew him. He was thinking something.

"But...well...it sure is dirty." He looked like he regretted saying so.

"Very dirty," Sally agreed. "But I have good friends to help clean."

Essley laughed when Darthrok's jaw dropped.

"What?" he asked. "You want me to push a broom? I'm a little more skilled than that. You could hire anyone to clean."

"Don't want just anyone here," Sally said. "Keeping it quiet."

"What about that thug Rex?" Essley asked. "Will he keep the secret?"

Sally bit her bottom lip, thinking. She had no real way to know what Rex would do. She just didn't know him well enough yet. "I hope so. If not...I'll kick him in the gasket."

Darthrok laughed along with Essley this time.

"Once we get it clean, then what?" Essley asked. "How

do we get the factory actually working again, now that it's all powered up?"

Sally had spent the past two days examining the place from top to bottom, and she knew she didn't have the necessary knowledge to get the factory going again on her own. Bringing it back to life had only been the first step.

"I'll bring Sujan here," she said. "He'll know."

Her friends stared at her.

"Sally," Essley said hesitantly. "He's not like you. He can't leave his store."

Sally had already thought a great deal about what she'd do if she managed to wake the factory up. Her journey had started with her own awakening, and she'd completed a quest here that no regular adventurers had managed. That had to mean she could do more. What else in Everternia could she bring to life?

She had some ideas.

"Not yet," Sally said. "But he will. I'll figure out how."

She'd learned a lot since she'd woken up. She learned more every day. Sujan and the factory were puzzles she could solve, if she kept working hard. And she would, because it was what she wanted. She wasn't someone who just did what was expected of her. Not anymore. She'd keep learning and adventuring and growing.

She was Sally Strong, and she was going to change the world, whether it was ready for her or not.

MESSAGE FROM THE AUTHOR

Thank you for reading! Sally is a very special character, and I'm glad to be able to share her with you. With everything going on in the world, I really needed to write something that was bright, shiny, and hopeful.

Reviews are critical to my being able to keep bringing you new books, so if you enjoyed this story and can spare a minute or two to leave a review on Amazon, I'd be grateful.

Please sign up for my newsletter at www.zendipi-etro.com to receive updates on new releases.

I hope to hear from you!

In gratitude,
    Zen DiPietro

ABOUT THE AUTHOR

I'm just looking for enjoyment and inspiration and characters to root for, just like you.

I like noodles and cats. I work hard. I dream a lot. I think in terms of how things could be rather than what they are. I like the word "if" because it changes everything. My best stories and art come from me asking "What if...?"

I like trying things. I like thinking and laughing. I like it when my cat doesn't attack my feet when I'm sleeping.

www.ZenDiPietro.com

OTHER WORKS BY ZEN DIPIETRO

Jiyu's Underworld Hit List

Dodging Fate series

Dodging Fate
Dodging Fate 2: Extra Fateful, Uber Dodgy

Hello Protocol for Dead Girls: A Virtual Awakening

The Dragonfire Station series

DRAGONFIRE STATION UNIVERSE

Original Series (complete)
Dragonfire Station Book 1: Translucid
Dragonfire Station Book 2: Fragments
Dragonfire Station Book 3: Coalescence

Intersections (Dragonfire Station Short
    Stories)

Mercenary Warfare series (complete)
Selling Out
Blood Money
Hell to Pay
Calculated Risk
Going for Broke

Chains of Command series (complete)
New Blood
Blood and Bone
Cut to the Bone
Out for Blood

To get updates on releases and sales, sign up for Zen's
newsletter.

www.ingramcontent.com/pod-product-compliance
Lightning Source LLC
Chambersburg PA
CBHW031718170626
46808CB00005B/1797